Whispering Winds

Whispering Winds
by
Randall Lane

"Oh my goodness!!! I just finished Devil's Den. What a roller coaster of a ride!!! I LOVED this book!! I can't wait to read your other stories, thanks again!!" — **Sherrie W Review for Devil's Den**

"This is not a book that I would have normally read, but I went to a reading by the author and was mesmerized by his incredible skill at drawing you in with sensational detail. I was right there in the story and was spellbound by this affecting and powerful book! The writing is excellent, the story is compelling, and the book has a message that touches your soul, one you will not forget! Looking forward to more from Randall Lane! I give the Devil's Den five big stars!" — **Janet B Review for Devil's Den**

"I loved Devil's Den. It was scary and quite intense as I read through it. I could not figure out, "who dun it." I really enjoy a book that has me guessing until the very end. I can't wait until your next novel is published! Thanks for such an enjoyable read." — **Sandra N Review for Devil's Den**

"I recommend this book highly. Devils Den. Can't put it down!"—**Marybeth L Review for Devil's Den**

"Awesome read! Once you start it's hard to put down! The way he tells the story keeps you captivated throughout the entire book." —**Tammy P Review for Devil's Den**

"I really enjoyed this book. The plot grew with an intense "who dun it" while surprising me with a twist I didn't anticipate. It's a great read in good vs. evil. You will find yourself questioning the validity of each character." — **Happy Amazon Customer's Review for Devil's Den**

"Mr. Lane writes with the eloquence of a storyteller. Deep, profound and superbly imaginative." — **Mark M Review for Devil's Den**

"This author's imagination will leave you spellbound! These stories will excite your senses, give you pause to think and excite your very soul! Can't wait for more!!!!" — **Happy Amazon Customer's Review for When Darkness Hides**

Table of Contents

2

"The Light shines in the darkness, and the darkness has not overcome it."

—John 1:5

Out Beyond the Pines

Devon Garrison's dream since childhood has been to venture deep into the secluded Blue Ridge Mountains on an extended camping and fishing trip. When a high-risk high-reward crypto bet paid off this past summer, Devon blocked out two weeks' time to check this coveted item off his bucket list.

The drive up from Florida had been long and exhausting but the reward waiting for him would make it all worth it. He arrived in Asheville late last night and stayed in a motel. He was up before the sunrise this morning and finds himself winding up a mountain towards his destination. The plan is to camp and live off grid for ten days. All the while hiking almost ten miles from various fishing spots he had scoped out and investigated through numerous online forms and YouTube videos.

His eighty-seven Ford Bronco crawls over the gravel as the pavement had ended long ago. Rocks ping against the undercarriage and wheel wells. The radio is tuned to a classic country station and ole Hank Williams moans out *Howling at the Moon.*

Fog slithers over the path as the headlights pierce into it. A swift breeze bends a few limbs and breaks off their leaves. Devon glances into the rearview mirror and sees orange and pink skies flooding the horizon as the sun shines through all the growth. He trains his eyes back on the road ahead and sees nothing but black sky as the night fights for another minute of power. A raccoon scurries across the path.

Devon smiles to himself and takes a deep breath to relish the moment. He would do anything if his brother Mike could have made the trip with him. The two had often talked about doing such a thing but were never able to get around to it. Mike died last May after a prolonged battle with ALS. Mike made Devon promise him he would take the fishing trip they had often talked about. Devon looked him in the eye and promised. If Mike hadn't of done that, truth be known, Devon may not have chosen to make the trip. He was torn. Part of him wanted to do it, but another part of him felt a little guilty for going without his brother.

He ran over a dip and the whole cab jiggled and squeaked. Devon lowered his foot onto the peddle and continued deeper into the mountains.

HE REACHED the checkpoint and eased the Bronco in front of the cedar hewed split rail fence near the visitor restrooms. He stepped out and gathered his gear, checking and rechecking everything as he went. He wore a Springfield XDM chambered in ten millimeter on his right hip and a hunting knife on his left. The Springfield had a capacity of sixteen rounds. The bullet entered like a quarter and exited like a cash register. He had enough fire power to bring down anything walking on two or four legs in the Northern Hemisphere two times over. He fitted into his heavy backpack, locked the Bronco, and headed for the trail.

Three wooden signs were nailed to a pine at the entrance. One said ½ mile to Devil's Pass, another said 3 miles to Crazy Woman Creek. The creek had received its name from a local folklore about an insane woman who had lived her whole life in the mountains before turning feral. She had lost her mind after her husband's passing. Legend says she's often heard wailing and moaning for her husband late into the night. There's countless tales of men being chased off the mountain from her piercing, hair raising screams. While interesting, Devon had never been one for any woo woo crap. The likely scenario was of course a mountain lion as they are known to sound strikingly similar to a woman in distress. Many Natives and early settlers thought the woods to be haunted and forbode anyone from meandering where the screams were heard. It wasn't some lonely ghost that Devon feared as much as it was a sneaky mountain lion creeping up behind him. Which was why he felt inclined to carry his Springfield.

His plan was to take his time hiking to Crazy Woman Creek, enjoy the scenery and fresh air, and make camp downriver at a place he heard was good for Rainbow Trout. It's there he plans to spend the day hunting for a big one. He'd head out in the morning for Johnathan's Creek which was another place known for good fishing.

Devon took out his cellphone and snapped a picture of the three signs. He sent it over to buddy and lady friend in Florida with a simple caption of:

Day 1 . . . Wish me luck!

He turned off his phone and slid it into a pocket in his backpack. A trio of crows began to caw overhead in a tall pine after he zipped it shut. The sun had risen enough to light the trail. Devon pulled his beanie further over his ears and blew into his hands. He clapped them together and huffed out a breath. He watched it steam into the cool morning air before beginning the trek to Crazy Woman Creek.

The leaves rustled to his right. He turned and watched a chubby squirrel dart up a pine tree with a mouthful of acorns. It climbed to a high branch and angled for its nest. Another squirrel sat on an even higher branch and barked down at Devon as he passed.

The woods grew thicker the further he travelled. The pines eventually gave away to gumball trees, oaks, and spruce. Hillside blueberry, black huckleberry, and mountain laurel take advantage of the sunlight filtering through scarce gaps between the tall trees. A vast assortment of birds sing and call to one another as they light from one branch to another. Every so often, Devon hears the cawing of crows above the chatter of the other birds. The crows follow him as he goes.

The trail steepens and turns a bit rocky. He trips once and nearly twists an ankle. That's the last thing he needs is to twist an ankle in the first hour of the trip. Wouldn't that be something? It would be his luck too.

As he nears the top of the incline, he hears people talking. Two heads poke above the horizon of the trail. He sees an older lady and gentleman with hiking sticks heading his way. He nods and says hello. The couple do the same.

The man and woman are the only people Devon sees along his journey to Crazy Woman Creek.

A LITTLE OVER an hour and a half later, he reached Crazy Woman Creek. By nine o'clock he had found his spot and set up camp. With his tent set, he turned his attention to rigging up his rod. He tied on a small, white rooster tail with black and yellow spots and a gold blade. The rippling water filled his ears and made him feel like a kid again in anticipation of catching the big one. He made his way down to the creek bank and quickly made the first cast from his spinning reel. He'd thought about taking fly fishing lessons but decided it would be more aggravating than it was worth and chose to stick to his old and trusted spinning reel. He'd caught more fish than he could count with it and figured it'd be enough to do the trick here in the creeks of Southern Appalachia.

He'd go on to spend the next three hours walking up and down the creek bank making his casts. By lunchtime he had enough trout for two meals. He'd also missed a nice one that stole his rooster tail. He'd cursed loudly when the line snapped. It was shortly after that incident when he felt the eerie feeling of being watched. It had settled over him like the shadow of a dark storm cloud. He made a few quick glances over each shoulder and scanned across the creek for any movement. He chuckled at himself and hurried to tie on another rooster tail. This one was yellow with black feathers. He finished tying the lure and went about making his casts. Devon tucked the thought and feeling of being watched deep into the far corners of his mind.

After getting back to camp, he made quick work of cleaning the two big Rainbows. He roasted them over a fire and saved the leftovers in a baggy for later. As he sat on log next to the fire, letting his lunch settle, he took solitude in observing nature and listening to the sounds. He'd brought along a small bird book and busied himself with identifying each one he saw. Most of them he could name without the book's help, but a handful had him stumped.

The Purple Finch and American Kestrel were two in particular he had never seen before and wouldn't have been able to name had it not been for the book.

With his lunch settling, he turned to store the booklet into his bag but was frozen in place when a high-pitched shrill cut through the air. Every hair on his body jolted upright and he felt a chill slither down his spine. His eyes flashed wide as he did a quick scan of his surroundings.

"What in the hell was that?"

As he questioned the sound, it did it again. Long, guttural, and yet piercing. It sounded like a woman being murdered. The screams lasted only for twenty seconds or so, but it was enough to send gooseflesh spreading across his body. He'd never heard anything like it in his life. He had lived in the Florida everglades for the last thirty years and had heard all sorts of wildlife late in the night. Even heard a wild panther in the swamps one time. Sure, it'd spooked him, but it hadn't had half the effect of whatever animal this was. His primal instinct had kicked into high gear and everything in him wanted to high tail it back down the mountain to the safety of his Bronco. He felt himself brace at the knees as his pulse soared. His fists clinched at his sides, and he began to smell his own body odor. His fight or flight mode was in full effect.

He swallowed hard and darted his eyes about his surroundings, waiting for it to scream again. With his right hand resting on the butt of the pistol by his hip, he chuckled and wagged his head. It was probably just a big mountain lion letting him know he was encroaching on its territory.

"I hear ya big guy. I don't mean ya no harm. I promise. You don't bother me, and I won't bother you, deal?" He said to the forest.

He smiled as he thought about all the stories he'd read and heard about grown men retreating off the mountain from that sound.

"A bunch of grown men scared of a big cat. Humph. What a bunch of wimps?" he said to himself as he patted his pistol. He gave a good scan of the woods before picking up his fishing rod and heading back to the creek.

HE WENT ON TO fish for another four hours. He caught three more of decent size. The biggest he decided to keep. He snapped a picture of it and sent it to his friends in Florida. He returned to his camp as the sun began to sink behind the trees. He built another fire and filled his gut with roasted trout once more. With his belly stuffed and his morale filled to the brink, he retrieved his grandpa's harmonica he had tucked away in his bag. He lay on his back by the fire with his head propped against a log and played some tunes on the harmonica. He knew *Oh Susanna* and *I'll Fly Away*. He could also play bits of *I Saw The Light* as well as *You Are My Sunshine*. He tried a few blues licks his grandpa had taught him when he gave the instrument to him one Christmas. He was never able to get it down pat though.

Man, Mike would have loved this.

He thought to himself after pocketing the harmonica and staring at the stars. He spotted the big and little dipper and was then able to find Orion's belt. His mind went back to his childhood when he and Mike used to climb on the roof of their father's building during summer nights and count the stars. After a while they started naming them also. Devon laughed as he remembered the name his brother had given one. Carl. For whatever reason, he used to think a star named Carl was the funniest thing. He finds himself chuckling now at the thought. He shakes his head and smiles. He felt a deep pain for his brother. Somehow though, he liked to think maybe he was with him here after all. He had no way of rationalizing the feeling, but somehow, he just knew. He could feel him. He reasoned it must be due to the love and memories he has for him.

After a while, Devon felt sleep begin to settle over him, so he stood and crossed for his tent. Not before putting out the fire with a before bed piss though. Moments later he was crawling into the tent and tucking into his warm sleeping bag. The sounds of nature flooded his ears. Over the rippling water of the creek and way off in the distance, he could hear a whip-poor-will. He loathed the thought of hearing the crazy woman. It sent a shiver down his spine at the recollection of that shrill. He hid away all the stories of haunted forest, creek devils, and mountain demons to the far reaches of his mind. He focused his mind on his childhood with his brother and fell asleep to the sound of water and whirring crickets.

HE DREAMED he was a kid again as he and his brother played in the woods pushing over dead trees. They laughed and hollered as each one fell with a thump. He watched through a blur as they must've pushed over a half dozen or more of these dead trees. After the last one fell, an even louder crash sounded behind them. Their laughter halted as they both spun towards the sound. They leaned down and peered through the forest towards the noise. All was quiet. Devon took a few steps forward. The leaves and twigs crunched beneath him. His brother stayed put. With his attention fixed to the spot of the loud crash, a branch snapped under his foot. At that exact moment he heard his brother begin to scream and a flurry of commotion rattled behind him. Devon's heart pounded and his blood turned to ice. He spun on his heels. The sight before him stalled his racing heart. Every hair on his body stiffened. His brother was being dragged from his hair through the woods by a huge, black figure with hulking shoulders and long, slender fingers.

As his mind tried to comprehend what his eyes were showing him, the monstrous beast let out a guttural howl.

At that, Devon jolted from his sleeping bag. His heart pounded so hard it made his chest ache. He panted for breath. Sweat trickled down his forehead and leaked into an eye. He wiped away the burn. He rubbed his face with both hands and took deep breaths. His heart began to slow, and he swallowed hard. He clinched his eyes and massaged his tear ducts.

A branch snapped somewhere out beyond the pines. Devon opened his eyes and raised his head. He listened to how quiet the woods were. Even the crickets were silent.

Another branch popped. Devon grasped in the darkness for his backpack. He danced his hand around a bit and found it. He unzipped it as quietly as he could. He felt for his Springfield and found it. He drew it out and gripped it tight.

Snap!

He jerked to the right. Another broken twig. How did it move over there so fast? Are there two of them? Two of what?

Leaves rustled behind him. He was being surrounded. But by what?

His heart skipped a beat when he heard something grunt followed by heavy breathing.

He adjusted his grip on the pistol and aimed it towards the sounds. More movement to his left this time. It wasn't a deer or anything on four legs. He could tell by the crunching leaves and sticks it was on two legs.

It stopped. Everything went silent.

He listened. Nothing. Just an eerie stillness.

The wind whispered through the pines and a pinecone fell to the earth. He flinched when he heard it drop. He scoffed at himself and listened again for more movement. Nothing.

He rubbed his forehead and checked his watch. "Damn, it's two o'clock in the morning. There ain't nothing out there, Devon. You're just spooking yourself." He said aloud.

No sooner than he finished his words, a glass shattering shrill blasted into the night. He clinched his teeth and winced. His chest vibrated from the noise. Leaves and sticks stirred as something began to run circles around his tent. He could hear heavy feet slapping and pounding the earth. It huffed for breath and grunted with every stride. A tall, wide shadow flashed by the tent. Devon rose to a squatted position and trained his gun to the shadow on the tent wall. He followed it as best he could as it dashed around his tent, grunting and huffing. Its breath rattled with a rasp, coming from a mucus filled throat.

Devon centered his aim on the daunting silhouette and pulled the trigger. The inside of his tent flashed white, and his ears rang from the blast. The silhouette disappeared the instant his bullet left the barrel. Silence filled the air.

Devon panted for breath and held his shaking gun at eye level. He cursed and blinked hard. He flexed his jaw as sound slowly crawled back to his ear drums. A quarter sized hole in his tent allowed a slimmer of moon light to filter through the opening.

In the far distance, he could hear a voice. A scream. A call for help. It was faint but grew louder with each cry. He stepped closer to the bullet hole in his tent, turned his ear and listened. It was his brother's voice. He jerked back and stared at the hole. He shook his head.

"No. No. No. This isn't real. This isn't happening." He pinched his arm and slapped his cheek. He felt it all. This is real.

Help! Devonnnn! Help me!

His brother's voice called for help, drawing out the words.

Devon beat the heel of his hand against his forehead. His brother continued to yell as he drew closer with each scream.

Devon grinded his molars and steadied himself. His breathing quickened. He crossed to the opening of his tent and made quick work of the zipper. He stepped through and planted his feet on the hard soil. The creek rippled down the bank. His brother's voice continued wailing.

With his gun gripped tight and in a ready position, he angled around his tent, stood at the back of it, and listened.

His brother's screams ceased.

He stood there for a moment longer.

All he could hear was the breeze playing on the leaves and the rippling creek. The forest was tomb quiet. He had that strong feeling of being watched again. Devon scanned the darkened woods, looking for something peering out from the cover of a tree. He searched for leering eyes but never found any.

He lowered his gun and looked up at the full moon. He saw a wispy cloud pass in front of it.

Snap!

Before he could lower his eyes in time to investigate the noise, the beast was upon him. He caught a glimpse of black, wavy hair. He thought he saw an antler or a tree branch near its huge head. He heard it growling and felt its hot breath against his face just before it sank its teeth into his neck. He heard it make slurping sounds as he felt his rib cage being torn open. His world turned black as he fell into a deep sleep.

THREE DAYS later Devon Garrison's camp was discovered by a group of hikers. Everything had been ransacked and torn to shreds. There was no trace of the man nor any drops of blood. His pistol and a boot were found a few yards from his tent. A spent shell casing was discovered inside the tent. Ballistic investigators were able to match it with the size of the hole on the tent wall. His friends and closest relatives were informed of his disappearance a week later. Devon's off and on girlfriend in Florida, Caroline Brown, had contacted the North Carolina police after she hadn't heard from Devon in three days. He'd promised to call or text once a day. Her last conversation with him was when he had sent pictures of the trout he'd caught on the first day. Her call had put a name and face to the missing man.

DNR and forest rangers launched a search that lasted for a total of five days but had come no closer to finding him than they had the day his camp was discovered.

Caroline Brown along with Devon's best friend, John Beaty, had spent the better part of a month researching missing people cases near the Blue Ridge and Appalachian Mountains. There were hundreds if not thousands of cases of hikers, hunters, fishermen, kids, you name it who had vanished over the years in that region. Following the internet rabbit hole, Caroline and John stumbled across everything from Bigfoot, serial killers, aliens, ghosts, and pretty much everything in between. One scenario stood out among the others though. It was a tale they had come across on more than one occasion. It was the story on the origin for the name of Crazy Woman Creek.

Caroline had remembered Devon joking once that he hoped he didn't get killed by the ghost of the lonely woman who was said to roam the hills near Crazy Woman Creek. He had only mentioned it in passing late one night after they had both had a few too many drinks. They laughed and joked about it, never saying any more on the subject.

Caroline dug deeper and eventually found another origin story behind the name. She discovered a YouTube video of an elderly Native man sitting on the front porch of a log cabin in a rocking chair. He had two long braids of hair over each shoulder and wore a brown hat with feathers stuck on the side. He leaned forward in his rocking chair and placed his hands atop a wooden cane with an eagle carved into it.

He said many men had heard the crazy woman over the years. None had ever claimed to have seen her and survived. The old man said there were countless stories of men who had been spooked while out in the woods by something they couldn't identify. It would start with the feeling of being watched. Like something was hovering over your shoulder and breathing down your neck. Then you would hear phantom footsteps nearby in the woods. Many even claimed to hear the cries of passed loved ones as the entity mimicked the voices of those close to the victims. Some men claimed to have caught glimpse of something huge and bulky in the corner of their eye, tearing through the woods after them. Wailing and screeching like a dying woman during the pursuit. Someone behind the camera asked the man what this creature was.

Caroline and John watched the old Native in the video turn his gaze from the mountains ahead and look dead into the camera.

"You have to be careful when talking about these sorts of things. You must be sure your heart is right with the Creator so you can have his full protection over you. The creature at Crazy Woman Creek is what us Natives know as a Wendigo. It's an evil entity that roams the woods in search of human flesh and spirit. Many believe it all started with a wicked medicine man shortly after we discovered the land. He was claimed to have lived in a cave deep in the mountains. He was a very large man and was often made fun of by the tribesmen. Though he healed many of their sicknesses, people were ungrateful for his help. He was visited one night by the devil himself who promised to seek revenge upon the people in exchange for the medicine man's soul. The medicine man was no match for the devil's charm and quickly agreed to the offer. Ever since, the wicked man has roamed the woods in search of sustenance. He is of his father the devil and has a way of deceiving many. He often mimics the voices of passed loved ones, children, or women in distress. He's not something you want to mess with."

The old man coughed and wiped his mouth with a handkerchief before continuing.

"I hear many people talking about the missing in these hills. I hear them say all sorts of crazy things as they wonder what may have gotten them. I don't wonder what happens to them. I know."

Caroline felt a shudder pass over her body at the thought of Devon encountering such a creature as the old man described. Is that what happened to him? Did he see it? It's now been three months since his disappearance, and it seems he'll be another number to add to the growing pile of victims.

Caroline raises her head from the laptop and looks at the wall in her office. It's covered in a six-foot by eight-foot map of the United States. She'd stuck various colored tacks across it and weaved string from one to another. She has over four hundred printed pictures of missing people pinned to the board. But that's only scratching the surface. She printed just a fraction of the stories she'd read online through news articles and blog posts. Some stories she'd read where hikers had disappeared from a group in mid hike. Many times, they'd even left their clothes behind on the trail. She remembered reading numerous times where the clothes were found neatly folded and stacked where the person had vanished seconds ago just behind the back of another hiker. Those stories always sent a cold shiver down her spine.

What's happening out there? Who or what is snatching up all these people?

She rubs her temple before downing a shot of scotch. She huffs out a breath and rises from her chair. She flicks off the lamp light and enters the hall for her bedroom. She lives in a small two-bedroom home with two acres of swamp land that backs up to a nature preserve. With the whole state of Florida having a warmer than usual winter, for the last week Caroline has slept with a window cracked in her bedroom.

She slides out of her house shoes and looks at the alarm clock on her nightstand. Red digital numbers reflect back at her. It's a quarter to two in the morning. She sighs and crawls beneath a thin sheet. She punches her pillow and rolls onto her side. Crickets chirp outside the window and an army of tree frogs screech into the night.

Her mind swims with stories she'd read and listened to online. She imagined being there with Devon when things happened. She forced her mind elsewhere and fought for sleep.

When she finally drifted into that dark place of nothingness, she thought she heard the distant cries of her missing boyfriend. She had entered that space of no return, and her mind convinced her she needed her sleep.

Besides, it must be part of some dream, right?

The Beach Bum

Gulls squawked overhead as they floated along in a swift ocean breeze. Waves beat against the slopping beach as they spread to caress the old man's toes. The sun peaked out from the horizon. Oscar Campbell caught a glimpse of a pelican in mid free fall as it searched for a morning pogie. The pelican diverted Oscar's mind from his dying wife, Abby.

She had fought and beat cervical cancer twice already and the stubborn thing had decided that wasn't enough. The evil beast came back last month with vengeance. Abby was given six months to live just yesterday. Oscar had cursed and called the doctor an unfriendly name. Abby had scolded him with one of her looks. She finished scolding him the rest of the way home from Wilmington. She had fought like a prize fight for the first two rounds, but this third bout had her seeming to accept defeat. Oscar loved her more than anything in the world, God as his witness, but the fact that woman was somehow okay with leaving this world in six short months had stirred an unusual anger in his heart. He kept reminding himself he should cherish every moment he had left with his wife and sweetheart since grade school, but he found himself with a case of resentment towards her he had to fight to ward from growing. He had argued with her and others more times in the last month than he had in the last decade. Abby had been his world for the last forty years of his life and they had travelled the country and globe together, raised three kids, and once ran an antique shop before the cancer took over their lives. The one place they never were able to make it to was Egypt. It had always been Abby's dream to see the pyramids and ride the back of a camel. They had booked an appointment with a travel advisor a week before the cancer returned. She was rushed to the hospital with stomach pain the day of the appointment. Oscar promised her she would see the pyramids.

"Come hell or high water, little lady you're going to see those pyramids."

He'd told her that as she sat in his lap on the recliner. He squeezed her tight and planted a big wet kiss on her forehead. She giggled that cute little giggle of hers and that was that.

They'd planned in the past to use a decent portion of their retirement account to spend on a month-long trip to the middle east. They'd planned to visit Egypt along with the Holy City of Jerusalem. Oscar didn't have the guts to tell her he'd lost the majority of their retirement funds making a risky bet on a small cap stock he'd read about from a Facebook ad. It was a semiconductor chip maker out of Massachusetts which was running for a couple bucks a share but was expecting to explode when China finally invaded Taiwan. Which so happens to be the king of semiconductor chips. With the king then dethroned, this little chip maker from good ole Massachusetts had its eyes on the prize, and so did their investors.

Oscar sold over eighty percent of their IRA and dumped it into this up and coming can't miss opportunity. That bet turned south quick when a month into it, the company's CEO was fired for sexual misconduct. The stock plummeted eighty-nine percent and has yet to make any attempt at a recovery.

A sharp stinging pain ripped through the bottom of his foot. The injury brought his mind back to the present. He winced and bent to tend to the wound. A broken seashell was to blame. The jagged edge had gouged right into the soft spot of his arch. He grimaced and rubbed at it. Fresh blood oozed into the sand. He removed a handkerchief from his pocket and tightened it around his foot. He dropped his flip flops onto the sand and slid into them. He grit his teeth and shook his head at his misfortune. He gave a quick side glance to the heavens and mumbled under his breath. If he listened hard enough, he imagined he could even hear the big man laughing at him. He sighed and turned around to head back to his truck parked two miles away at the end of the road.

Something on the other side of the dune caught his attention. A white trash bag rattled in the wind. He squinted and removed his sunglasses.

What the hell?

A boat tailed Grackle hopped upon the sand near the bag before squawking and taking to the air. Oscar stepped forward for a better look at the odd object. He felt his heart knock when the rest of the trash bag came into view. It was partially hidden next to a shrub, but the shape of it sent a ghostly hand caressing the back of Oscar's neck. He gulped as his brow furrowed. It can't be what he thinks it is, can it? He began to check his surroundings. He was all alone. He had only seen a few people this morning when he started his walk. They had all been down the beach in the opposite direction he had chosen to go. The bag rattled again as it was brought to life with the breeze.

He crept closer, keeping his eyes peeled along the way. The bag was long and slender with black electrical tape wrapped around it in three places.

"Good Lord, this can't be."

It has to be some sort of evil prank by mischievous teenagers. It has to be, right? There's no way he just stumbled upon a dead body. No way.

His mind raced with a million thoughts as it tried to convince him why this can't be happening. Somehow, he knew in his gut he was in the presence of the deceased. He could just sense it in his spirit.

He angled next to the bag and stood over it for a moment. He nudged it with his foot. It gave slightly and rolled back into place. If it is what he thinks it is, they hadn't been dead long enough for rigor mortis to set in. He peered over the dune and looked again for any beach goers. No one was around. He drew a deep breath and took out his Swiss army knife. He grunted when he bent down to slice open the plastic. The slit spread to reveal the pallid, gray face of a man who was left in the middle of a scream. His eyes were glazed like a fish, and he had salt and peppered stubble.

Oscar jerked back with a yelp. He nearly tripped over his own feet. He placed his hands on his head and panted for breath.

"Oh Jesus. Oh Jesus. No. No. This can't be happening."

He retrieved his cell phone and walked back to the body. With his phone in hand, he was about to dial the three magic numbers before he noticed something in the man's mouth. It was white. He leaned closer. It looks like a folded note. He grimaces and growls at himself. One side of his brain screamed to leave the body and scene alone for investigators to deal with while the other side just had to know what this note was all about. He straightened his spine and looked again over the dune to see if anyone was coming. The coast is clear. He leans back down and reaches out a timid hand toward the dead man's mouth.

The damp paper touches his fingers. He snatches back as if the man were about to bite him. He gently unfolds the note and begins to read. Four words are written in thick swirly letters: *LOOK AT MY TOE.*

Oscar squints his eyes and glares at the note then glares at the dead man. He looks towards the man's feet and makes a small cut in the plastic. Investigators will wonder why he made two cuts. He could easily explain the first as the curiosity had gotten the best of him, but the second cut would need a little more thought. He'll think of something to say later. He tears the plastic away to find two lifeless feet bound together with rope. On one toe hangs a folded tag. Oscar opens the note.

Text this number for instructions to the money. $1 mill if you bury the body in your back yard. Up for the challenge?

Oscar stared at the note. He read over the words at least a dozen times, trying to soak it all in. Finally, he began to laugh. His shoulders hitched. Tears filled his eyes. He placed a hand to his hip and the other to the bridge of his nose. He sucked in a gust of air and looked heavenward.

"Oh, that's a good one. You almost had me there for a minute."

He lowered his eyes back to the body and crossed over to it. He chuckled along the way and said, "Look man, I'm assuming my brother put you up to this shit. That was a good one. You can get up now. You got me."

He kicked the man's legs.

Nothing.

Oscar sighed and said, "C'mon, quit yanking my chain. You ain't no dead man. I know Ronnie put you up to it somehow. The joke's over."

As much as he tried to rationalize it all as a twisted prank put on by his childish brother Ronnie, the thought didn't really make sense when he let it sit in his mind for a moment. How would his brother had known he was going for a walk this morning? Of course, there's the fact that it's not unusual for him to do so, but how did Ronnie know he would be here at this exact moment? Better yet, how did he know this is where he would turn around at after stepping on that damned seashell back there? He wouldn't have. Which only means one thing . . . this ain't no joke.

Oscar's eyes widened at the thought. He swallowed hard and nudged the body again. This time with more force. The dead man remained dead.

"Oh Jesus, he ain't playing."

He drew closer and bent over the man to feel for a pulse. He couldn't get anything at the neck, so he tried his wrist. The flesh was cold to the touch and no thump ever came. The man was dead as a frozen fish.

Oscar scratched his chin and chewed on the inside of his lip. He took another look at the note.

Text this number for instructions to the money. $1 mill if you bury the body in your back yard. Up for the challenge?

He shook his head.

"This is silly."

He retrieved his phone and texted the number. He punched in three simple letters: *Hey.*

He lowered his phone and looked out at the rising sun as it glistened off the water's surface. His phone vibrated. He flinched. He looked at the screen. The number had texted back.

Wise choice old timer...

Those words pierced his heart like fangs from a rattle snake. He felt their venom seep into his blood stream, poisoning it with fear.

"How does he know I'm an old timer?"

Oscar jerked around, looking in every direction for prying eyes. The phone buzzed again.

It's a simple proposal. You take care of me. I take care of you. You bury this body. I pay you $1 mill. Up for the challenge?

Another text came in on the heels of that one. It read:

You should stop jerking around before you hurt yourself. I can see you, but you'll never see me. Don't believe me? You're wearing Blue Jeans with a red and black checkered button-down shirt. Short sleeve. You have black sunglasses and a tan straw hat. I had hoped someone younger would have come along to make things easier, but hey I always enjoy rooting for an underdog. Think you're up to it old man?

Oscar's breath had ceased. His heart had dropped to the pit of his gut. He felt it thump against his colon to almost cause an instant bowel movement. With trembling hands he struggled to keep from dropping his phone. His eyes scanned the beach across the inlet. It was empty. He blinked and looked at the houses in the distance. Even with a young man's sight it would have been difficult to see anyone, let alone with a seventy-six-year old's eyes. He turned around and looked behind himself. He scanned the trees and shrubs. Nothing. He looked up over the dune once more to the beach front. He even looked skyward for a spying drone. He was all alone.

He focused back on his phone. The stranger's words glared back at him.

A bead of sweat trickled into his eye. He blinked and wiped it away. His trembling thumb began to text.

ThIs Has to be a jok. How do i know your for reel?

A moment passed and the phone rattled in his hand.

Does this help?

Below the words was a picture of ammo cans full of banded ten-thousand-dollar stacks.

Oscar gulped and felt his heart flutter at the sight. He licked his lips as his pupils dilated. His pulse soared at the thought of what that million dollars could do for him and Abby. Hell, they could spend the rest of her life in Egypt if she chose to. They could even afford better doctors and treatment who may be able to extend her time on this earth. And all he has to do is find a way to bury this old feller in his back yard to earn all that? Why this is the easiest decision he's ever had to make. He could cut Ronnie in on it too to be sure it gets done. He would need some help anyhow and Ronnie was about the only person he could trust to help him. He could never drag the body back to his truck without being seen. His eyes lingered to the inlet. His brother does have a boat.

Another text came through.

What will it be old man? Are you up for it or should I wait for another?

Oscar rubbed his Adam's Apple and thought for a moment.

He texted back: *I'll do it but not without a 10% deposit. I'll need my brother's help to do this without getting caught. You leave $100k in the trash can at the boat landing. You put it in McDonalds bags. He gets the money and drives his boat over here to help with the body. No deposit. No deal.*

It took him a few minutes to type it all out and he read it over more than once. He chewed on his lip until he tasted blood. He scratched the back of his neck. He hit send before he could talk himself out of it. He removed his hat and ran his hand through his hair.

It seemed like an eternity had passed before his phone buzzed again.

Deal

"Oh my God, what am I getting into?"

He scrolled through his contacts and found Ronnie. His brother answered with a groggy tone on the fourth ring.

"Ronnie, I need to ask a favor of you."

AS OSCAR HAD expected, Ronnie thought it was all a joke. It wasn't until he heard the shake to Oscar's voice that he came to understand the predicament. He argued at first with Oscar that he should contact the police and not take the risk the stranger was offering. Oscar was able to change his mind by offering to go in fifty fifty with the money. Ronnie had always been the slightly more level-headed of the two, but like Oscar, he had a weak spot for money. Within ten minutes, Oscar had persuaded him to chip in. Being the avid fisherman that he is, Oscar's brother owned a twenty-foot center console they often went deep sea fishing with. On board the boat is a YETI 350 cooler perfect for storing the days catch. Or in this case, hiding a body.

Thirty minutes or more passed before Oscar heard his brother strolling up the inlet. The half hour felt more like seven days as he spent the entire time peeking over the dunes and checking the thin wood line behind him for any witnesses. When he finally saw his brother's boat angling around the bend, Oscar marched towards the beach and scanned for any early morning scrollers. The coast is clear. For now, at least.

His brother beached the boat and angled to the cooler in front of the steering wheel. He opened the lid then walked to the front and tossed out an anchor. Oscar watched it sink into the soft sand. He glanced up and down the beach once more and did a quick scan of the homes across the inlet. He rubbed the back of his neck and chewed on a lip.

"This is crazy, Osc."

Oscar nodded as he watched Ronnie hop down from the boat after killing the engine.

"Yeah, but you willingly agreed to it, didn't you?"

Ronnie arched his brows and tilted his head.

"If we get caught, this was all your idea."

"I figured you'd say something like that. Do you have the cash?"

Ronnie let a sly grin stretch his face, "All hundred k of it. I just hope it's all real."

Oscar swallowed as he rubbed his palms and looked around. He turned for the dune which hid the body.

"C'mon. Let's make this quick." Oscar said as he and Ronnie headed for the body.

They climbed the incline and stepped behind the dune.

"Oh my God," Ronnie said as the white trash bag came into view, "Shit, you weren't kidding."

"Did it sound like I was kidding?" Oscar said as he bent and grabbed the feet. "You're younger and stronger, you get the head and shoulders."

Ronnie cursed again as he strained lifting the body. Together, the two took three stumbling steps. Oscar lost his grip and the legs smacked into the sand. Ronnie grimaced as the jolt likely jarred his back.

Oscar regripped.

They started off again.

Oscar could feel sweat beading on his face as the biting flies began to swarm. He blew air towards his nose to ward them off. Not before he took two good bites near his eye. He blinked and scrunched his nose to try and relieve the itch.

About that time, Ronnie began cussing again.

"Those damned things biting you too?"

"Yeah."

"It's those no see ums. The wind dies down any at all and those things come out in droves."

Oscar felt one pierce the flesh on the back of his neck.

"Hold up a second. Let's stop right here. Let me check the beach one more time."

Oscar dropped his end of the body and scratched his face and neck. He caught a glimpse of Ronnie scratching too.

Oscar walked down to the beach and scanned it before looking across the inlet. Nothing.

He came back to Ronnie and the body. Oscar gripped the legs with a grunt.

"We good?"

"Good as we'll ever be."

A million thoughts flashed through his mind, but all he could picture was Abby riding a camel with a pyramid in the background. That image gave him strength and helped him rationalize his crazy plan.

The two struggled and stumbled, almost dropping the body more than once before hefting it up onto the bow of the boat. The dead man smacked into the floor once they shoved him over the side wall. Ronnie climbed aboard while Oscar panted for breath with his hands to his knees. His heart was beating harder than he had ever felt before. The carotid artery in his neck thumped like a plucked bass string. His lungs burned as they groaned for precious oxygen.

I swear if I have a gosh darn heart attack, I'm going to poke somebody in the eye when I get to heaven.

Ronnie's voice called out to him.

Oscar drew two deep breaths and rubbed his face before straightening his spine. Saltwater pooled around his ankles and soiled his socks.

"Huh?"

"I say hurry up and get your ass in the boat before someone comes around that bend. Get up here and help me put this ole sucker in the cooler."

"Well, you'll have to help me in the boat first."

Ronnie angled to him and stretched out his hand. They locked forearms, and Ronnie pulled him on board. They took each end of the body again and heaved it into the cooler. Oscar snapped the lid shut. Ronnie crossed to the front and began pulling in the anchor he'd tossed out to the sand. Once he had it in, he manned the stern and went to turn over the engine.

Oscar sat in the passenger seat still trying to catch his breath.

The engine growled but struggled to turn over.

Oscar watched Ronnie's Adam's Apple bob.

Ronnie hit it again. Same thing.

Oscar glared at his brother. Ronnie turned his head toward him slowly like an owl.

"It'll turnover this time. Sometimes it takes three tries."

Oscar clinched his teeth and angled his brows at his brother.

The last thing they need is to be stranded on the beach with a dead body in their fishing cooler. That'd sure be a hard one to explain.

Ronnie turned the ignition. The engine roared to life.

"We're in business," said Ronnie.

He threw it in reverse and moments later they entered the ICW and headed for the boat ramp.

This might just work after all.

Oscar thought to himself as he sat behind the captain's glass with the wind hitting the top of his head, sending his curly gray locks flapping behind him. He held his straw hat in his lap.

The sun beamed off the water as ocean spray lit his lips. He saw the picture in his mind's eye again of Abby at the pyramids.

I'm gonna get you there honey. You're gonna see those pyramids.

He mumbled to her.

About that time, a siren sounded off. His heart skipped a beat as it locked up in his chest.

No way. Please, don't let that be what I think it is.

He turned around to find flashing red and blue lights. The siren went off again. It's a Game Warden.

Oscar looked up to Ronnie and they met eyes. Neither said a word, their shared look said enough. Ronnie eased back on the throttle and began to pull out of the boat channel as he angled near the bank.

Oscar's heart began that unfamiliar thump again. His fingers trembled as he hid it by gripping tighter to his hat.

Ronnie eased to a halt. The DNR boat slid up next to them.

"How we doing there fellas?"

Oscar and Ronnie nod before returning the gesture.

"You were going a little fast back there weren't ya?" One game warden asked as he gripped the metal pole on the center console. Another warden stayed behind the wheel and watched the brothers closely behind his dark shades.

"Was I?"

The warden nodded, "Yeah, but that's not the reason we stopped you."

"It wasn't?"

"No. We were sitting back there—"

Oscar's pulse quickened at those words.

They've been caught. The wardens saw what they did. They had to.

"When you went roaring past us. I noticed it didn't look like you had a registration sticker." The warden pushed his glasses up and pointed at the side of Ronnie's boat. "I see I was right."

Oscar's shoulders slumped in relief. Those words were like music to his ears. Oscar watched Ronnie lean over the boat to have a look for himself.

"Why hell, that stupid thing just won't stay on. I tried glue and tape, you name it. I guess that sucker must've fell off this morning."

"Mm hm. You fellas do any fishing while you were out?" the warden asked with his eyes lingering to the cooler.

Oscar began to stutter as Ronnie looked to him for help.

"No. No sir. We—"

Ronnie cut him off and said, "We've been working on the fuel pump on this thing for the last week. It's been a real devil, I tell ya. We finally got it working though so we wanted to give her a test spin this morning."

Oscar chimed in with, "Yeah, we plan to go out this afternoon when the tide and winds turn. We prefer fishing an incoming tide."

The warden bobbed his head as he soaked in their words. Finally, after glaring at the cooler long enough, he said, "Yeah, me too. My granddaddy was the same way. The winds and tides can make or break a fisherman."

Ronnie nodded, "You got that right."

"Alright, well listen. You guys have been gentlemen, so I'm gonna let you go with just a verbal warning."

Oscar exhaled for what felt like the first time in this whole ordeal.

"But if I see you out here again without that sticker..." the warden lowered his head and angled his eyes. "I'm gonna get ya. Fair enough?"

Oscar and Ronnie couldn't nod any faster.

"Alright, you men enjoy the rest of your day and good luck later."

Oscar and Ronnie offered their thanks and parted ways with the wardens.

It was just after eight o'clock when they reached the boat landing. They had two hours before Abby would be up and wondering where her husband was. He hadn't told her about taking a walk on the beach this morning. That was something he decided to do after being woken at five worrying and thinking about their situation. If he was lucky, she might sleep till eleven, but worse case he had until at least ten. Which he figured would give him and Ronnie enough time to bury the man without her ever knowing. He planned to cover it up by planting the garden atop him. He knows how sick and twisted it is, and even Ronnie protested his choice, but it's the perfect disguise. Oscar and Abby had talked just last week about it being time to get the old tiller out and churn up some dirt. What better day to till a garden than the day you've been tasked with burying a dead man in your back yard?

Ronnie eased his truck and trailer into Oscar's driveway, and they made their way around back. Oscar got out and peeked into the bedroom window. He was relieved to find Abby sleeping with her back to him. He crossed to Ronnie and the two climbed into the boat to gather the body.

An hour later, and plenty blisters to show for, the two had dug a big enough hole to lower a casket into. Oscar climbed out and wiped the sweat from his brow. Ronnie placed his hands to his hips and leaned to crack his back. Oscar rubbed the blood blisters on his palms and grimaced.

Ronnie sighed and said, "Who the hell is this guy anyway?"

"I don't know, and I don't want to know. I think it's best that way."

"Yeah, but ain't it like shooting a man when he's not looking at ya or something? Won't he come back to haunt ya or something like that?"

"Shut up, Ronnie. Let's just get this over with. C'mon, help me roll him into the hole."

Ronnie shook his head and tightened his lips.

The two dropped the man into the hole. He landed with a hard thump. If he was alive, it'd likely knocked the breath from his lungs.

Oscar retrieved his phone and was in the process of snapping a photo when a voice called out from behind them. He nearly tossed his phone in the air.

"Honey? What're y'all doing out there?"

The sound of Abby's voice sent him leaping out of his flesh. He spun around to find Abby standing on the back porch, a silhouette behind the black screen. He cut his eyes to Ronnie then looked at the shovel. Ronnie got the message and started shoveling dirt onto the body. Oscar crossed the yard and started yapping up a lie.

"Hey sweetie. Yeah, Ronnie caught some fish this morning. We buried the scraps beneath where I'm going to plant the garden. It'll make the ground nice and fertile."

He watched Abbey wrinkle her nose before squinting her eyes at him to question the idea. He opened the screen door and gave her a kiss before taking her in his arms.

"Really? He went fishing without you?"

Oscar searched for words.

"Uh, yeah can you believe it? That sorry rascal. I guess he felt guilty, so he thought he'd offer to help with the garden. He only caught three fish. They weren't all that big. He offered me one, but I told him he could keep em."

"Well, at least he offered it." She waved at Ronnie, and he waved back. "That's an awful big hole, isn't it?"

Oscar gulped. "Well, you know, I mean we had to make sure the scraps were deep enough in the ground so an animal wouldn't try digging them up."

"Hmph. Well, I'm going to make some coffee. You want one cup or two?"

"I'll take just one." He kissed her again and watched her go back inside.

He whistled out a breath and thanked the heavens. He went out the screen door. It slammed behind him. He picked up a shovel and helped Ronnie cover the hole.

Twenty minutes later the job was done. Two blood blisters had popped on Oscar's palm. Another bled in the crevice of his thumb and forefinger. He sucked on the wound and watched Ronnie wipe his brow with the back of his arm. Oscar walked to his building and pulled out the tiller. Half an hour later, he'd done enough to cover the recent hole. He shut the engine off and took out his handkerchief to dab the sweat on his face.

"Now what?" His brother asked.

"I guess I text this feller back and show proof of what we did. He's supposed to send instructions or a map for the rest of the money."

Oscar pulled out his cell and began texting.

Ronnie scratched the back of his neck and wrinkled his face as he peered at Oscar, "Makes ya wonder what in the world this guy did to be worth a million dollar cover up, doesn't it?"

Oscar waved him off and said, "Oh don't go talking like that. All that matters is we did our part. Worse case at least we're both fifty grand richer than yesterday, right?"

"I guess."

Oscar looked up from his phone and squinted at his brother. "You guess? What the hell you mean 'you guess?'"

"I mean what if we're being set up somehow? You don't know who's on the other end of that phone." Ronnie pointed to the device in Oscar's hand. "Hell, that could be the Mafia, the Southern Gentlemen, a Clinton hired hand…what if shit goes sideways and they come after us for something?"

"Ronnie, it's too late for all that. We're in deep and they ain't no getting out now. The least we can do is make sure things follow through so we can get the rest of this money. Can you imagine what you could do with five hundred k of cold hard cash? C'mon, Ronnie. We've come this far, they ain't no turning back now."

"I'm not talking about turning back, I'm just saying we gonna have to be watching our backs from here on out less we end up like the feller we just buried in your backyard."

Oscar nodded and sent the text.

A moment later his phone buzzed.

Nicely done! I knew you had it in you.

Oscar responded with, *Okay, now what about the instructions for the $???*

Ronnie came close and hovered over his shoulder as they glared at the screen.

Patience my fellow man. Patience. I was just getting to that. See the attached map.

Another text came through right after that one. It was a hand drawn map of marshland and tidal creeks. A single black line snaked its way through the marsh to what looked like a large tree. A bright red X sat at the base of the tree.

Just like any old pirate story, X marks the spot. Here you will find seven sealed ammo cans with the reward. Thank you for your business. Maybe we can do it again sometime.

"I know where that's at. Look there's the old church that burned down and right there's Dink's service station." Ronnie said as he pointed at Oscar's phone.

"Yeah, I think you're right."

"Look, if we drive here in the boat we could enter the marshland there. That's a shorter walk than going at it from the parking lot at that public fishing dock. Plus, there would be less chance of us being seen with all those ammo cans."

Oscar thought about it.

"That's a good idea but remember you ain't got no registration sticker on ya boat. If that warden sees us again, he'll hall our asses to jail."

Ronnie cursed and stomped the ground.

"But hey, we could park over here. Ain't there that old dirt road that runs out beside Dink's? If I remember right, it seems like oyster hunters used that road for years before the DNR shut it down after that bad algae bloom one year."

"Hey, yeah that's right. I forgot about that. It's pretty secluded too. Yeah, that'll work. I'll drop the boat off and we can ride up in there."

"Alright then, let's hit the road."

"What about Abby? Won't she be wondering what you're doing?"

"Yeah, I'll just tell her you and me went up to the store to get some tomato plants."

"Alright then, well hurry your ass up."

Oscar turned and marched to the back porch. He opened the back door and yelled for Abby. He told her the plan and said goodbye.

Twenty minutes later, after the two unloaded Ronnie's boat back at his house, they were winding up the old dirt road, inching closer to the treasure.

Oscar stared at his phone. That big, red X glared back at him.

The truck bounced as Ronnie did his best to dodge the potholes and miss the branches hanging out into the path.

Oscar kept checking the mirrors to be sure they weren't being followed. He saw Ronnie doing the same.

The path began to open up a bit as the marshland came into view. The sun glistened off the tidal creeks beyond the tall Spartina grass. A narrow trail cut through the weeds and grass and led to the big live oak standing in the center. There were no houses or boats anywhere in sight. Just like Ronnie had said, it's pretty secluded out here.

Ronnie parked his truck and the two stared out the window for a moment. They checked all their surroundings for any ambush or lookeylews.

Satisfied that the coast was clear, they climbed out of the truck. Oscar checked his phone once more to verify they were at the right spot. There's no denying it. This is where the money is.

They began their trek towards the live oak and stole glances over their shoulders the whole way. The stench of decomposition filled the air the closer they got to the marsh. The live oak stood on the last of the hard soil and fifty yards from there was where the creeks began.

Gulls flew overhead and called to one another. The air was hot and thick with humidity. A dark storm cloud formed near the horizon as it grumbled its way toward the vast Atlantic.

The live oak came into full view and so did the army green ammo cans sitting at its base.

"Fried monkey on a stick, the stupid bastard left a million dollars just sitting in the shade of an oak? Who the hell does that sort of thing?" Ronnie said with bewilderment.

"The same sort of guy who pays a million dollars for an old man to bury a dead body in his backyard I reckon." Oscar replied.

They stood under the oak and glared at the ammo cans. Oscar scanned around one last time before bending down to open a can. After a slight struggle with his arthritic fingers, he was able to pry the can open. He pulled the lid back and felt his heart leap at the sight of banded, crisp Benjamin's looking back at him. He craned his head up to Ronnie and smiled as he took out a wad and flipped through it. The air lighting on his cheeks.

"Well, I'll be damned." Ronnie said.

Oscar and Ronnie checked the other cans and were delighted to find them much the same way.

After two quick trips, they'd loaded all seven ammo cans of cash into the truck and were hightailing it out of there.

On the way back, Ronnie dropped Oscar off at the beach so he could pick his car up from where he'd parked it earlier for his morning walk. Oscar followed Ronnie back to his house where the two took the cans inside and divided it out. All one million was accounted when you included the hundred k they already had. They eyed the bills carefully and even compared them to bills of their own but were unable to spot any differences. They googled ways to spot counterfeit money and tried every trick they could find, but each one they did only verified the authenticity.

Satisfied, Oscar took his share, gave Ronnie a brotherly hug with a slap on the back and headed home to Abby. He grinned like a schoolboy with his first crush most of the way home until he heard something in the back seat of his car. Climbing the hill towards home, he chuckled to himself before glancing into the rearview mirror. He screamed and jerked the wheel. The dead man sat in the back seat smiling from ear to ear. His flesh was ashy gray and decaying as worms slithered out from his teeth and nostrils.

Oscar's car fishtailed and the wheel yanked violently out from his grip. A guardrail with a bright yellow sign warning of the sharp curve ahead, rushed towards him. Oscar's heart pounded as his mind shouted at what lied on the other side of that guardrail. It was at least a fifty-foot drop straight onto a rocky shoreline with crashing waves.

The dead man began to let out a deep, knee slapping, belly aching laugh and Oscar watched his shoulders hitch in the mirror. He tried to correct the wheel, but the guardrail only came faster. His car smashed through it and took a nosedive for the rocks. The dead man's laugh grew louder in Oscar's ears until gravity finished its job and the car crumbled like a piece of tin foil into the rocks.

Cash floated with the breeze as Oscar's spirit joined the dead man in the afterlife.

Bloody Bones

57 miles West of Wilmington, NC
Winter of 1893

Arthur and Josephine Rice live in a quaint, three-bedroom home with cedar shake exterior and an outhouse in the back yard. The married couple has raised four children so far, with a fifth on the way. Arthur's elderly and alcoholic mother has lived with them for the last two years after his father's death. Arthur and Josephine are seated at the kitchen table. An oil lantern with a weak flame light their faces. It's just passed the midnight hour, and all four children and Arthur's mother had long since turned in for the night. Arthur sat in his white long johns and rested his elbows upon the table. He looked into Josephine's eyes as he spoke.

"Look, we have enough food to last for four weeks. That'll give me time to go into town and work a job long enough to get us through the winter. I read in the paper there's a new textile mill hiring."

"I don't know Arthur. That's a long time for you to be away. Isn't there something you can do that's closer to home?"

She watched as Arthur lowered his gaze and tightened his lips, "I wish they were. This textile mill thing is about all I know of." He raised his head and pointed toward the field behind their house, "If we hadn't of had such a terrible drought this year, we wouldn't be having to think like this. I's was talking to Old Man Rigsby last week and he say it was the worst one he seen yet. You and me both know he done seen his share of years."

Josephine hugged herself and shivered. The thought of Arthur leaving them sent her stomach rolling.

Arthur rose from the table and crossed to the pile of firewood next to the wood stove in the living area. The iron door creaked open, and he tossed in a log. Embers danced as the flame licked at the fresh wood.

"You would have enough food and supplies for four weeks. I double checked." He shut the door and rose to his feet.

Josephine sighed.

"What is it?" He asked her as he drew near.

She shook her head and looked away.

"No. Now c'mon, don't be like this Josey. What's on your mind?"

She looked back at him as if questioning whether he really wanted to hear her thoughts.

"Why go on. Let it out."

"I don't want to be here that long with your mother. It's bad enough when you're working out in the field all day. You know me and her ain't the best of friends."

"Aww please. Josey, you'll be fine. She's not that bad."

"That's easy for you to say, you're not the daughter-in-law that's never good enough for her."

"Now Josey, you know there ain't no truth to that. I know she might have an odd way of showing it, but she really does think a lot of you."

Josephine wrinkled her nose and gave a bewildered glare.

"Okay, well maybe she doesn't think a lot of you, but she does think of you."

Josephine slapped his chest and the two shared a laugh as he took her in his arms. He kissed her neck and said, "You'll be fine. Trust me."

Josephine agreed to Arthur's plan. Three weeks later she came to regret the decision. She hated herself with passion each time she heard the voice of one of her children crying out with hunger pains. Arthur had undoubtedly miscalculated their oat and grain supply by a wide margin. Josephine had rationed it out as best she knew how, but they were now down to one meal a day and would soon be lucky to have that. Josephine had created a makeshift hog trap yesterday morning. She and Arthur's mother, Margaret, had argued over its effectiveness most of the day. It'd never be strong enough to kill a hog, Margaret had protested. Josephine had watched her father kill many a hog using the very trap. She knew good and well that it'd kill a hog. The question was not whether it'd work, but whether a hog could be found in what was beginning to feel a lot like a barren wasteland.

The children cried and begged for supper. Even the baby kicked and squirmed within her. No doubt feeling the lack of sustenance.

Margaret had been short tempered all day and often lashed out at the children. Josephine had all she could take at one point and told Margaret if she didn't control herself, she'd kick her out to fend for herself. Margaret snickered and said something about it being a cold day in hell before she'd let her daughter-in-law do such a thing. Despite her dismissiveness of Josephine's words, Margaret never raised her voice at the children again.

Josephine rounded up the last of the grain and oats and did her best to make a meal. She returned to her room afterward with a growling stomach as she only allowed herself enough to keep the baby healthy and nothing more. Had it not been for the baby in her womb, she would have fasted before eating what could have gone to her children. She was skimpy with Margaret's portion too and the two argued over it for most of the meal. Her disdain for that woman was only growing by the hour.

As she knelt by the bed to pray, her mother-in-law called for her from her bedroom. Josephine ignored her for a moment and continued praying to the Almighty. At last, Margaret's voice irritated her more than nails across a chalk board. She finished her prayers with a huff and asked for forgiveness. She rose to her feet and crossed for Margaret's room. The door was slightly cracked, and Josephine nudged it open.

"What is it?" she asked with an edge to her tone.

"Step in here for a moment."

Josephine eyed her suspiciously, wondering where this was leading. She stepped in and shut the door.

Margaret drew a deep breath and stood with her arms crossed at the foot of the bed. She rested her hip against the medal frame.

"You disrespected me back there, little lady."

Josephine batted her eyes and tilted her head. "I beg your pardon?"

"You heard me. I didn't stutter."

"Margaret, I don't have time for this. There are more important things to tend to." She turned and aimed for the door.

Margaret rushed her and grabbed her arm.

"Don't you walk away from me when I'm speaking to you," Margaret growled through clinched teeth.

Josephine yanked from her grip and Margaret lost her footing. Josephine watched it all as if it were in slow motion. Margaret stumbled head long, full force into the door. Her temple thudded against the heavy, metal handle. Josephine gasped and placed her hands to her mouth. She watched as a deep laceration formed across Margaret's head. Blood gushed and spurted out. Her eyes were glossy and dazed like a stuffed animal.

Josephine stared in shock at the sight before her. Margaret didn't move or bat an eye. She was as good as dead.

Oh my God.

Josephine stepped closer and squatted down to check for a pulse. She never found one. Margaret was gone.

IT HAD TAKEN Arthur a week longer to return home than he'd expected. In his four and a half weeks of working at the new textile mill, Arthur earned enough wages to buy food to last through winter and on into spring. He had made the trip to and from Wilmington on horseback along with three other men. He'd departed from those men an hour earlier and is now only minutes from home as he trudges along the narrow path. Trees line the edges and hang over the trail like arms stretching forth to snatch someone up.

Arthur smiled as a giddiness filled his spirit. He couldn't wait to tell Josephine the news and show her the money he'd earned. They may even have enough left over to buy her and the children new clothes. He clicked his teeth and nudged the horse forward.

Their home came into view. Smoke billowed from the chimney, and he thought he caught a faint whiff of stewed meat.

He'd worried for the last two weeks how his family was doing with the food he'd left behind. The past week had weighed heavily on his mind as he feared what the extra week may have done. He trusted Josephine would ration things as best she could until he returned. His thoughts were swept away at the sight of his four children playing in the front yard by the swing beneath the tall oak.

His two younger daughters, ages five and seven, glanced up and began running towards him. Their tattered dresses were dingy at the bottom from dragging the dirt and in desperate need of a good wash. John and Gabriel, the older of the four, were close behind their sisters.

Arthur hurried forward to meet them. He hopped from the horse and squatted to a knee as all four of his kids rushed to wrap their arms around him. He squeezed them tight and kissed each one on the top of the head.

"Oh my goodness. I'm so glad to see you."

He was ecstatic to see the energy they exhumed. He'd long feared everyone would be weak with starvation and shriveled in bed. Praise God Almighty, that isn't the case. They each beamed with joy and life.

They pulled back from him, and he asked, "Where's your mother?"

John pointed to the house and said, "She's inside. She's cooking supper."

"What is she cooking? Does she have meat?"

"Hmm mmm. It's so good too."

"Where did she get it?"

"Mama said she caught a hog in her trap last week. We've been feeding off it ever since. We ran out of food about three weeks after you left. We were all starving until she got that hog."

"Is that right?"

Mary, the youngest daughter, mumbled, "It's so so good."

"Mmm, it sure smells good. How is your grandma?"

"She's been staying in her room a lot. Mama said she's been sick and running a fever. She doesn't want us near her. Said we might catch something." Said John.

Arthur rose to his feet and walked towards the house with the reins of his horse in one hand and Mary's hand in the other.

He reached the porch and tied his horse to the railing. He removed his hat and stepped inside.

The house was dark as it was lit only by a dim lantern.

He scanned the darkness to find Josephine standing in the kitchen with her back to him. Her arm stirred a pot of stew.

He crossed toward her, "Hey honey. I'm so sorry it took me so long to get back."

She didn't acknowledge him but continued to stir the pot.

He walked up behind her and squeezed her waist, kissing her neck and cheek. She didn't respond. He pulled away and stepped to the side to look at her. Her eyes were distant and glossed over. Her hand worked vigorously to stir the stew. He swallowed hard and batted his eyes.

"Honey? Are you okay?"

She gave a gentle nod.

"Hey. What's the matter with you?"

"They were starving. We all were. The old hog has kept us alive." She had yet to blink.

Arthur squinted at her and said, "So I heard."

"Its meat is really tender and moist. You'll love it."

He took hold of her arm and gave it a shake.

"Hey. Honey? Josey? Are you alright? What's going o—"

She blinked hard and snapped her head side to side. She cleared her throat and finally looked at him. The distant stare had left, and his Josey had returned. She hugged him tight and began to cry. They embraced for a moment.

Arthur pulled her head to his shoulder. She wept as she sunk her nails into his back.

"I didn't think you were coming back. I thought something happened to you." she said with hitches and gasps for air.

"Sshh. Sshh. I'm sorry honey. I'm sorry. It's okay. You're alright now. I'm here."

She sniffled and pulled back.

He wiped the tears from her eyes.

"I have some good news to share. Where's Ma? Is she in her room?"

Arthur stepped from Josey and headed for his mother's room.

Josey grasped at his hand and called out, "No. Wait. WAIT."

Arthur had already reached his mother's room and had his hand on the doorknob. It was locked.

He turned to Josey who had marched up next to him, and said, "What the hell is this? Why is her door locked?"

Josey only gave a blank expression. He watched a shadow cross her face as the blood drained from her flesh.

He turned to the door and began to knock and call for his mother. No answer.

He rammed his shoulder into the door.

Josey clung to his arm and pleaded with him to stop. He shrugged her off and continued banging against the door. The children had now huddled around their mother.

Finally, the door gave way and Arthur stumbled into the room. He was instantly smacked in the face with an acrid odor that stung his nostrils and made his eyes water.

He buried his face into the crevice of an elbow. He turned and glared at Josey who stood in the door frame, trembling.

He turned back and scanned the room. The bed was empty. The covers were pulled back and ruffled into a ball near the foot of the bed.

"Ma?"

Nothing.

"MA?"

Josephine had tears dripping down her cheeks, "I'm sorry, Arthur. I'm so so sorry."

"What have you done?"

In frantic desperation, he began searching the room.

He crouched and checked under the bed. There was nothing there. He straightened and crossed for the closet door.

"Wait. Arthur. No, I can explain."

He turned and looked at her. Tears puddled to the floor at her feet, and she covered her mouth with her hands. The children were also crying and clinging to their mother.

Arthur gulped and turned to the closet door. He took hold of the handle. He heard something shift behind the door when he began to open it. He worked past his fears and yanked the door. It swung open and out spilled the decaying body of his mother.

The children screamed.

Arthur yelped and leaped backwards.

Her forehead had a large gash and was shaded with a ghastly bruise. Her mouth was drooped open in a drawl. Her eyes were sunken deep within their sockets.

His heart banged like a drum as his pulse quickened. His eyes fixed to his mother's arms and legs. Large chunks of meat were missing. A thought flashed across his mind as the words of his oldest son, John, screamed in his head:

Mama said she caught a hog in her trap last week. We've been feeding off it ever since. We ran out of food about three weeks after you left. We were all starving until she got that hog.

"Dear Jesus, what have you done, Josey?"

He turned to look at her. Her shoulders sagged. Her voice cracked as she said, "It was an accident, I swear. We would have starved, Arthur. I didn't know what else to do."

57 miles West of Wilmington, NC
Present Day

MARIA FAULKNER had been saving for a down payment on a home for the last three years. She and her nine-year old son, Sammy, have lived in an apartment ever since they lost their home to foreclosure when her husband died. Maria spent countless hours combing every Zillow, Realtor, and Craigslist ad she could find. Yesterday she stumbled upon a nice, new doublewide sitting on two acres of land well within her budget. She wasted no time calling the buyer's agent she and her husband had used in the past.

She signed the necessary agency agreements and scheduled a showing later that day.

"So, this one is a two bed two bath. It comes in just shy of fifteen hundred square feet. There are luxury vinyl flooring throughout, and as you can see, you have brand-new stainless-steel appliances," her agent said as she gave Maria and Sammy a tour.

Sammy clung to her side while working on a blue sucker. Maria noticed he seemed particularly fixated on the closet of what would be his bedroom. He'd locked eyes on it the second they stepped into the room. Almost as if he'd heard or saw something. She felt him grip her arm tighter when her agent opened the closet door.

Maria rubbed her hand through his hair and patted his back.

"It's okay sweetie. There's nothing to be afraid of. See. It's just a closet. Look how big this room is. You'll have twice the space here as we do at the apartment." Maria says to him.

Her agent smiles and waves her hands throughout the closet. "I remember I used to be scared of closets too when I was a kid. I bet even your mom was at one time."

"I sure was."

"I remember my mom said she had Bloody Bones when she was growing up. My grandma used to tell her that Bloody Bones was going to get her and her brothers if they didn't behave." The agent whispers past the side of her hand to Sammy, "It was just scare tactic kid. There's no such thing as monsters in closets. There all just as empty as this one. Here's your proof."

Sammy still stares at the closet.

"I'll bet you're a big Lego guy aren't ya? Huh? I just bet you are."

She looks at Maria and grins.

"He hasn't spoken since Sean died on deployment. That was three years ago."

The agent places her hand to her heart and says, "Oh my God. I'm so sorry to hear that."

"Thank you. Yeah, he was just starting to talk before Sean was sent to Iraq for a second tour. His doctors say couple his autism along with such a traumatic event at a young age, may lead to him never speaking again."

The agent squeezes Maria's arm and says, "I'm so sorry. Maria, you are strong woman to endure what you have. You're doing amazing. Sean would be so proud of you."

Maria sniffled and said, "Thank you. I try my best. That's all I can do."

Maria would go on to get an offer accepted on the property and a month later she and Sammy were moving in.

On the day of the move, with boxes scattered through the home and furniture quickly arranged in the living room, Maria and her best friend, Brittany, spend the evening chatting and sipping red wine as Sammy plays with Legos in the floor.

"You guys are going to love it here. This is so much better than the apartment. Like look at how much more space you have. And you have two acres too. Girl, you hit the jackpot with this place."

"Thank you. Yeah, I knew I couldn't pass this one up once the numbers made sense. I just have to get Sammy to overcome his fear of the closet. He's never been that way before, but for whatever reason, that closet in his room gives him the creeps or something. He sort of creeped me out the day of the showing."

"Really? What do you mean?" Brittany asks with a chuckle before sipping more wine. She crosses her legs like an Indian and turns toward Maria as they sit on opposite ends of the couch.

"I don't know. He's just going through a phase, I guess. I mean all this is new to him, you know. A few years ago, when Sean was still here, he went through a stage where he was afraid there was a monster under the bed. He'd go around saying, 'Monk monk. Monk monk,' and pointing under every bed."

Brittany laughed and said, "I remember that. He did that at my house a few times too."

"Yeah, he did, didn't he?"

The two continued chatting for another half hour before calling it a night. They hugged and said their goodbyes. Maria and Sammy stood on the front porch and watched Brittany back out of the driveway. After waving her off, Maria turned to Sammy and said, "You ready to tryout your new bed?"

Maria read to Sammy from the Adventures of Tom Sawyer, and within twenty minutes he was fast asleep. She laid in bed with him for another ten minutes or so to be sure he was out, before planting her feet to the floor. She flicked off his lamp and crossed for the door. She watched him for a moment as she peered through the darkness. Maria smiled and let out a sigh before easing the door shut.

IN HIS DREAM, he was sailing down the river on a homemade raft. The wind brushed his hair back and water splashed his face. Something rattled loudly but he could never place where the sound was coming from. It reminded him of the antlers his dad used when he took him deer hunting. He had watched him clank and rattle them together from the tree stand or blind. That is what the sound reminded him of. His dream began to fade as reality blended in to confuse the two states of consciousness.

The dream turned to darkness with a faint red hue as he stared at the back of his eyelids. The sound of rattling bones continued. He flashed opened his eyes and jolted up in bed. The bed sheets were thrown to the foot of the bed during his movement. His breath came in short gasps. He blinked as he tried to peer through the darkness. The rattling came once more. It ceased when his eyes fell on the closet. The folding doors were left open as he had begged his mom not to close them.

All he could see was the faint outcropping of a few shirts hanging in place. Then his heart knocked. He swore he could make out a face staring back at him. He fumbled for the flashlight on his nightstand. He found it and brought it to his chest. The bone rattling started again. He struggled to find the on switch for a second. He panted for breath and felt himself wet the bed. He started to whimper before finally switching on the light. He jerked it to the open closet. Nothing. Just clothes.

The light winked, flickered, then burned out.

He smacked the side of it, but it never came back to life. He remembered the night vision option on his iPad's camera. It lay on the nightstand next to him. He reached over and snatched it. He flipped over the cover. The screen burned his eyes for a moment. He swiped to the camera and clicked a few buttons before the screen turned black and white. He angled the iPad to his closet and held it there. The hanging clothes came into picture. It was blurry at first, but then the lens focused. Something round drew his attention. He felt his pulse rachet up again as he slowly began making out the features of a face. The nose. The lips. The eyebrows. THE EYES! The lids flashed opened to reveal bright white eyes. The lips pulled back to show big white teeth. The figure hissed and rushed from the closet with its bony hands outstretched for him.

He gasped and tossed the iPad. He yanked the covers over his head and clinched them tight within his little hands. The bone rattling sound filled the room again.

His whole body quivered. His bladder released a deluge. He felt the bed sink beneath something's weight near his feet. The thing's breath was raspy and smelled like sewage.

He could feel it crawling closer towards him. The bed squeaked with the added weight. He drew a deep breath and yelled with all he had in him.

He didn't stop yelling until something yanked the cover from him and turned on the lamp light. It was his mama. She hugged him tight and tried to console him.

He wept and pointed at the closet.

"Sshh. Sshh. It's okay. I'm here, honey. I'm here."

She rocked him in her arms as he clung tightly to her. After a few moments, Sammy finally began to settle. She stood and walked with him back to her room. She changed him out of his soiled clothes and sang to him until he fell asleep in her bed.

THE NEXT DAY she called Brittany to tell of their first night. Brittany mentioned she had an aunt who claimed to be a medium. She said she could come out and walk around the property to see if anything was going on. At least to ease Maria's mind a bit. She was hesitant at first, but since it was her friend's aunt, she gave in and agreed for Brittany to schedule an appointment.

The next day around noon, Brittany and her aunt, Valerie, pulled into the driveway.

Maria watched from the window as Brittany helped her aunt out of the car. She was a heavy-set lady with long gray hair and by the looks of it suffered greatly with bad knees and hips. She walked with a wooden cane to help with the hitch in her step. She wore numerous necklaces and bracelets. Brittany helped her towards the door. Maria watched her stop in her tracks after only taking a few steps.

Maria stepped out onto the front porch with Sammy clinging to her side.

"Hey Britt."

Brittany looked at her and placed a shushing finger to her lips. Maria looked on as her aunt Valerie scanned the land with squinted eyes.

A breeze rustled the leaves and birds sang while hopping from one branch to another. A dog barked in the distance followed by the crow of a confused rooster.

Finally, the lady broke her gaze and spoke, "There's a dark energy here. Something tragic has taken place upon this land. It weighs heavy on my spirit. I can feel it." The last two sentences she said while looking at Maria.

Maria's mouth went dry. She licked her lips and swallowed. She cleared her throat and added, "I'm not sure how to respond to that, but my name is Maria Faulkner. This is my son Sammy. I appreciate you agreeing to come out here on such short notice."

Valerie nodded and said with a tight smile, "It's a pleasure to meet you both. When Brittany told me this morning about your son's condition and behavior, I felt it was important for me to visit to see for myself. My instinct has always served me well, and from the moment we pulled into the driveway I could sense something was off about this place."

"I don't understand," Maria said with a wry smile and tilt of her head before continuing, "This is a new house. No one has ever lived here before."

"Your thinking's all wrong ma'am. Houses are not the only things that can be haunted. This here dirt is older than all of us combined. Something has happened here. It's not the house, but the land it sits upon."

"But why us? Why would anything want something to do with us?"

"Children like your son are exceptionally sensitive and vulnerable to the spirit realm. As are the young and elderly. Animals too. A dark spirit may attempt to attach itself to your son to draw from his light. Every dark being craves the light within such pure individuals. It will often intimidate or harass the pure and vulnerable to push them into a weakened state so it can draw from that light."

Maria sighed and rubbed her tear ducts.

"Do you mind if I have a walk around the property?"

Maria waved her around and said, "Be my guest."

The four of them angled for the back yard. The old lady's jewelry jingled when she walked. Once they rounded the corner of the house, Valerie stopped and scanned the land again. Maria watched her closely. After a few minutes the old lady grimaced before closing her eyes and swaying in place. She dropped her cane as her hands balled into fists. Brittany took hold of an arm and motioned for Maria to grab the other. The old lady rocked side to side while mumbling incoherently under her breath. This went on for five minutes or more. It ended when the lady slumped and dropped her head towards the ground. Her body hung limp for a moment before jolting straight. The old lady began an ear-piercing wail. She shook violently in Maria and Brittany's arms.

Brittany consoled her and patted her on the cheek. Maria watched Valerie's eyes flash wide as she panted for breath. She took hold of Maria and Brittany's hands, squeezing tight.

"Sshh. You're okay Aunt Valerie. We got you. We're here. Easy now. Catch your breath."

Sensing she was beginning to settle down, Maria stepped away to be with Sammy who stood to the side with wide eyes. Maria embraced her son as Brittany helped Valerie come to her senses.

From a dry throat came a cracking voice, "It's a female spirit. Her name is Margaret. She's haughty and narcissistic. I don't know what happened to her, but she feels she was wronged and defiled at her death. She is a vengeful and bitter spirit. I believe she had grandchildren in her lifetime, but she despised them and considered them a nuisance. I believe that may be why she has been giving your son trouble. She is strongly connected to closets. I don't know why that is the case, but there is something about closets that she is connected to."

Maria's mind instantly went back to the real estate agent's mention of the folklore her grandmother believed in. Maybe there was something to it.

Valerie stepped close to Maria and took her by the hand. She looked deeply in her eyes and said, "You will need to stand up to her and rule over her. You have to assert your dominance with her, or she will with you. She must know she has picked the wrong child to terrorize."

"Are you sure about all of this?"

"As sure as I've ever been in my life. I would advise making a salt perimeter around the entire house and make a line at the front and back doors. You may want to cover up your mirrors for the next few days as well, just to be sure you close off any portal in case she tries to bring along other spirits."

"My God, should I call a preacher or something to bless the place?"

"It certainly wouldn't hurt."

That night Maria had Sammy sleep in her bed. She left all the lights on throughout the house and kept the closet doors open. She'd also done as Valerie had said about the salt. A preacher from the local Freewill Baptist Church was scheduled for a visit tomorrow.

Sammy had stayed awake with her for most of the night while keeping a watchful eye on the closet. Maria reassured him numerous times that everything would be okay. Mama was here now.

It must've been around midnight when Sammy finally drifted to sleep. Maria wasn't far behind. She dreamed of a family beach trip much like the one they had taken shortly before her husband's death.

As she entered that distant land between dream and reality, she began to hear noises. It started as a faint creak like the working of a rusty door hinge waving in the wind. Then it turned into a horsed whisper with a raspy undertone. Her dream of the beach quickly faded to black as the gravelly whispers grew louder. They begin to be accompanied by the sound of rattling bones. She felt herself stir as she swam to the surface of consciousness. She opened her eyes. The room was pitch black. Her nose felt like an icicle. Her cheeks stung as if she were walking in a blizzard. She watched as her breath steamed into the darkness. The bones continued to rattle, and something began to growl.

She tossed the covers back and felt for Sammy. Her hand hit the mattress. The space next to her was empty. Her heart leaped into her throat. She found him sitting up in bed with his gaze fixed towards the closet. Her eyes went there too. A silhouette formed in the darkness. She stared until the features came into picture. She could see the shape of a woman's face with long hair and bony hands stretching for her son. The woman growled as her bones creaked and rattled.

Maria jolted to her feet and shouted at the spirit. Margaret snapped her head around and hissed. Maria snatched Sammy from the bed and held him close to her side. The old hag roared. Her bones clattered together.

"Go away. You hear me? You're not welcome here. This is my house. This is my land. THIS IS MY SON!"

The spirit let out a long, piercing wail before something popped as air rushed in to replace where she once stood. The lights flickered and hummed before coming to life. The temperature of the room returned to normal. Maria squeezed her son and kissed his head.

"It's okay sweetie. Mommy's here."

The next morning Maria called and told Brittany of their experience.

The first thing Maria said when Brittany answered was, "Well, I think I got rid of Bloody Bones."

That she did. Margaret never returned after that night. That isn't to say Maria hasn't caught herself checking the closets from time to time or bolting awake every time something goes bump in the night. So far, those bumps have been nothing more than the house settling or a branch tapping a window. It would be nice if things stayed that way.

Lie Bumps

Georgetown, SC
1965

Doug Clemmons drove his red Chevy Impala along the dirt road. He grimaced at the sound of rocks pinging off the under carriage. He glanced in the rearview mirror and saw a thick dust trail as he angled his way towards the prospect's home. If he'd known they lived on such a long dirt road, he'd have waited about shining the tires. All that work he'd put into cleaning the car over the weekend would be for nothing after he left this place. Doug shifted his eyes to himself and extended his tongue. The bump was still there. He rolled his tongue over his bottom right canine. A flash of hot pain flared, and he winced. His mind travelled back to the last time he'd seen the dentist. It must've been some twenty years ago when he had his wisdom teeth removed. That was an experience he'd prefer to forget. He'd promised himself he'd never visit a dentist again. But does a dentist deal with tongue bumps? He thought about it for a minute before shrugging and picking his nose.

The road began to snake to the right as an immense cornfield came into view. A scarecrow hung like Christ in the center. Only it wore a potato sack on its head rather than a crown of thorns. Beyond the field, Doug took in the farmer's home. It was a large white, plantation style home with a weathered wrap around porch. The white paint had flaked in multiple spots along the shake siding. A big red barn was to the left with a green tractor parked inside. An old man and woman sat in rocking chairs on the front porch. The scene reminded him of something Norman Rockwell would enjoy looking at.

He eased his Impala into the driveway and passed their leaning mailbox as he did so. The farmer sipped on a glass of tea and offered a nod and wave. Doug returned the gesture and turned down the Elvis tune playing over his radio. He shifted into park and killed the engine. His bulky briefcase full of cookware was stationed in the back seat along with all the sales pamphlets and order forms. Doug stepped out of his vehicle and retrieved what he needed before crossing to the steps of the porch.

"How you do Mr. and Mrs. Wilson?"

Mr. Wilson narrowed his eyes and drew a breath as he sized Doug up from top to bottom. He cleared his throat and sat his glass of tea down on the table next to him.

"Wasn't sure you'd come out here after our last discussion."

"Well, Mr. Wilson, I'm a man of my word. Here I am." Doug said with a smile and ta da motion of his arms.

He looked to Mrs. Wilson whose eyes were glued to the briefcase like a kid staring at a lollipop. Doug grinned and said, "It's a beautiful day out, isn't it?" He didn't wait for an answer but gave his attention to the tractor out in the barn. "That John Deere you have out there, is that a Waterloo Boy?"

"It sure is. I see you know your tractors."

Doug smiled and grunted, "My grandfather had one just like it. His was a 1923 model I believe. I had a toy of it when I was a kid. It's in my office now as we speak."

The effort to build rapport seemed to work as he could see Mr. Wilsons eyes soften just a bit.

"Well, I don't want to hold you any longer than needed. How today is going to go is I'm going to ask a few more questions to get to know more about your situation. After that, I'll explain the different products we offer and how we do business here at Arthur's Cookware and what makes us different. At the end of all that, if I feel we are a good fit for one another and that our products can be beneficial to you, I'll extend an offer for us to do business together. All I need from you at that point is a simple yes or no. Sound fair enough?"

He received blank glares from the old man and woman.

Doug held the silence and forced the old man to finally answer.

"You said something like that last time."

"Yes sir, but you didn't let me finish. If you recall, you stopped me short when you said you were going to your truck to get your scatter gun."

Mrs. Wilson grinned and said, "He didn't mean nothing by it. It's just we've dealt with so many travelling salesmen who just try to take our money. We've seen everything from vacuums, Bibles, television sets, life insurance, you name it. We figured you were just another slimy salesman looking to take advantage of the elderly."

"Well, I can certainly understand why you would feel that way. You are not the only folks I've come across who have felt the same way. But what I have found is that most of them have never encountered a professional salesman who was not trying to sell them anything, but simply offering a solution to the problem they face. My obligation and duty isn't to get you to buy but to help you solve the problem of over spending on less than par cookware. If I could show you a way to save time, energy, and money by getting a great deal on a set of cookware that will be guaranteed to last five times longer than what you currently own, is that something you would be interested in?"

Mrs. Wilson looks at her husband, and they hold eyes for a moment. The two look back at him and the old man says, "If I find out you're just yanking our chains, I'll have my scatter gun pointed at your chest faster than you Yankee boy can say you all. That understood?"

Doug says with a smile, "I'm actually born and raised here in good ole South Carolina, sir. I don't say you all, I say y'all. But yes, that is understood."

"Well, you sure don't seem like it to me."

"Do you mind if we talk in the kitchen for a few minutes?"

The old man dug at some wax in his ear and studied the specimen on his fingertips for a second before answering.

"Bertha, you may want to put some coffee on. I have a sneaking suspicion this'll take more than a few minutes."

"I assure you both it won't take anymore time than necessary."

With that, the Wilsons rose from their rockers and headed for the front door. The old man opened and held the door for his wife. He motioned for Doug to follow.

"Name's Frank by the way. Wife's is Bertha May, but everyone calls her Bertha. You don't have to call us Mr. and Mrs. and all that fancy bullshit." Frank said while holding the screen door open.

Doug nodded and stepped inside with his briefcase.

A victrola played a Buck Owens record somewhere in the shadows. The faint aroma of sweet bread wafted through the air. A curved staircase spiraled to the left. An office door was off the bottom of the stairs. Straight ahead was the kitchen. To the right was the dining room. Buck Owens grew louder as they entered the kitchen. Off from the kitchen was the living area with a sofa, recliner, Magnavox Console TV with wood trim, and the source of the music. A hip height Victrola with horn and crank sat against the wall next to the television. Doug smiled as it reminded him of the one his mother owned. She loved to play Elvis and Chuck Berry on it. Their house was always rocking.

Doug pulled himself from the memory and fixed his eyes on the bar in the kitchen. He raised his briefcase and angled his chin, "May I?"

"Oh yes. Go ahead. Here let me move this pan out of your way." Bertha said as she cleaned off the area.

Doug placed his briefcase atop the bar and popped the locks. He opened it carefully as if it contained a million dollars. Bertha looked on with eager anticipation. He laid the lid back and let the sparkling pots and pans and silverware do their talking. He withdrew the flyers and pamphlets and began his sales presentation.

A half hour later, they'd retreated to the living area for coffee. An hour afterwards and four cups of coffee deep, Doug had convinced Bertha her need for his pots and pans. Frank on the other hand needed a little more selling to. Bertha tugged on his arm and pointed out all the features and qualities that Doug had presented. Frank only sat there chewing on a toothpick, not saying a word. He drilled his steely blue eyes into Doug's soul and prodded.

"We can't afford it. Your prices are too high. Simple as that."

Bertha groaned. "Oh Frank. Don't be like that."

Yeah. Don't be like that Frank. Doug thought.

"Okay. I hear what you're saying but let me ask you this, Frank. Is it price or cost that you're concerned about?"

Frank arched his brows.

Doug looked at Bertha and asked, "Miss Bertha, how many sets of cookware would you say you have purchased in the last five years?"

She chuckled and looked at the floor, "Oh goodness. I'd say half a dozen maybe. I pretty much buy a new set each year because that's about all the life I get out of 'em. I use 'em every day, so they wear out pretty quick."

"Uh huh. And how much would you say you paid for each set?"

"I don't know. Maybe twenty or thirty? Something like that."

"So would you agree then that over the course of the last five years, you've likely already spent a hundred to a hundred and fifty dollars on cookware?"

Bertha looked at Frank then at Doug. She nodded and said, "Yeah, that sounds about right."

"Okay, so based on what you're telling me, I'd say you're focusing on the price of my product when you should be focusing on the cost of my product."

"What's that supposed to mean?" Frank asked with an edge in his voice.

"The price of my product is thirty-nine ninety-nine. Which is higher than what you usually pay for your cookware, would you agree?"

They both nodded.

"However, the cost of my product is much less than what you have already spent in the last five years on your cookware."

"How is that?" Frank asked.

"Because our cookware comes with a five-year guarantee or your money back. So basically, by purchasing my cookware, yes, you may pay a little extra on the price today, but the long-term costs of my cookware are far less expensive than what you are currently spending. Does that idea make sense to you?"

They only stared at him.

"The way I see it. You have two choices. You can continue buying a new set of cookware each year or you can pay an extra ten to twenty dollars now but save yourselves roughly a hundred dollars over the next five years. You catch my drift?"

"Hmph. But how do I know you're not lying about how long those pots and pans last?"

"Well...let me show something Frank." Doug said as he opened up his blazer and dug into his inner pocket. He pulled out a folded stack of paper. On the eight by eleven sheets were the handwritten testimonials of past clients. He opened the papers and sat them down on the coffee table before smoothing out the center crease.

"Take a minute to read over these reviews. I'm going to excuse myself to the restroom if you don't mind."

"Go right ahead honey. It's down the hall. First door on your right."

"Thank you. I won't be just a moment."

Frank held the papers in front of him and looked down his nose through his coke bottle glasses.

"Now hold up a second partner. How do I know you didn't just write all this shit up this morning? How do I know these are real people?"

"Well Frank, I have their telephone numbers right there. You are more than welcome to give them a call. I'm sure they'll be happy to speak with you."

Frank tightened his lips and fixed his eyes on Doug.

"There's a few farmers on that list too. I'm sure you'll have lots to talk about. Please excuse me for a moment."

Doug left the room and wiped his brow. The bump on his tongue pounded like a thumb struck by a hammer. He reached the bathroom and locked the door. He looked in the mirror and stretched out his tongue. The bump had grown to the size of a steel bb. It was red with a white center and hot with fever. He gently touched it with his finger and sucked in air through his teeth as a flash of pain spread across his tongue.

Damn it.

A tear welled in the corner of his eye, and he drew a deep breath.

He pulled away from the mirror and undid his fly. His bladder thanked him for the kind gesture, and he flushed and lowered the seat when he was finished.

As he made his way back down the hall, he heard Frank speaking to someone on the phone. He'd entered the kitchen and stood by the landline attached to the wall.

The old doubtful rascal.

Doug smiled as he passed him.

Frank only glared as he questioned the person on the other line about the legitimacy of Doug's cookware.

Doug sat across from Bertha who was busy looking over the pots and pans.

"Do you have any questions for me at this point, Miss Bertha?"

He watched her give his question some thought before looking up at him and saying, "You know, come to think of it, I do."

"Hit me."

"I see here it says thirty-nine ninety-nine including shipping and handling."

"Uh huh."

"What if I buy this exact set from you? Wouldn't that save the shipping and handling cost?"

He heard Frank hang up the telephone before making his way back from the kitchen.

Doug cleared his throat and adjusted in his seat. He wiped his leg as if swiping off a crumb.

"Well now, that is certainly a possibility Bertha. However, you had told me earlier you wanted this cookware set in pearl white. Are you sure you would prefer the sterling silver over the pearl?"

She looked at Frank then at the cookware.

"What y'all talking about?" Frank asked.

"Bertha here was trying to shave off the shipping and handling charge by settling for my model here rather than the pearl white as she originally wanted."

Frank grunted, "Makes no difference to me as long as the food tastes the same. Would be nice to save a few bucks though if it's possible, I reckon."

The shipping and handling charge Bertha was trying to save was actually where a large portion of Doug's commission stemmed from. It would be a cold day in hell before he reduced his commission like that. If she wanted his display model, then by golly she can have it. The extra chunk of his commission would be a different story. If this was the route she wanted to go, he'd offer to let her have it for half down and the other half due next month. Of course, she would still be charged the shipping and handling fee. Only it would be labeled as a sneaky little interest charge. Bertha gets her cookware. Doug gets his full commission. Tada and abracadabra.

"I tell you folks what...I'll let you have the cookware today for half down. You try it out for thirty days and if you're not completely satisfied, you get your money back. But since I know that won't be the case, we can go ahead and set you up on a payment plan for the other payment which will be due exactly thirty days from now. If you want to cancel, give me a call, I rip up the agreement and will pick up the cookware the same day. Sound fair enough?"

The two looked at each other for a long moment.

Realizing defeat, Frank turned away and huffed.

Bertha looked at Doug and said with a wide grin, "Deal."

They forgot to ask how much the second payment would be.

Doug was out the door and on his way to Charleston before it ever crossed their minds. He crunk up a Muddy Waters song and cruised the interstate for his next appointment. All the while his tongue throbbed like the devil. He was beginning to wonder if a spider had snuck into his mouth last night and stole a bite or something. When he exited the interstate and came to a stop sign, he glanced at himself in the mirror. His heart knocked when he noticed another red bump festering beside the first one.

He cursed and growled.

He had gotten the pestering rascals before but never this bad. This time around was like a hornet had been given free range to roam about his tongue, poking here and there whenever he pleased.

He went through the four way stop and continued towards Main St. His stomach begged for feeding, so when he caught sight of the drive-in diner with a big rotating burger above it, he couldn't resist.

He gave his order to the cute blonde and returned to checking his tongue in the mirror. He had the sudden feeling of being watched. He turned to find an old man and woman staring from the car next to him.

He smiled and shrugged his shoulder, "Doc said it may be rabies."

The man scowled and looked away.

Doug chuckled and went back to examining the bumps. They seemed bigger now than when he was at the stop sign only half hour ago.

What in the hell is happening?

He tried mashing the bumps between his fingers like he was popping a pimple, but the pain was extraordinary. He wiped a tear leaking from the corner of his eye and growled as he pulled away from the mirror.

He rested his arm on the window seal and waited for his burger. The Beach Boys sang *Help me, Rhonda* over the outdoor speakers. The girl comes back with his food. He has to eat on one side of his mouth to avoid the bumps on his tongue. He finishes up and throws his trash away. He sits back into his seat and heads for the interstate. An hour later he'd reached a small, country town by the name of Huger. His prospect, Eileen Fuller, was a seventy-year-old lady who had called the cookware ad in the paper two days prior. After taking a few side roads from town, Doug found himself travelling down a long, narrow road with live oaks on either side. The Spanish Moss hanging over the road looked like melted skin dripping from the tree branches. Doug counted two houses in the last ten minutes along the road. One looked abandoned, the other looked like it was well on its way.

He approached a sharp left curve. Straightening out of it, a white mobile home came into view. It sat on the right-hand side near the road. There was no underpinning so the concreate blocks it sat on were visible. It had red shutters and a red porch. An old 40's model Ford was tucked away to the side within a tall patch of grass and weeds. Free ranging chickens roamed about, pecking at the ground. Three young children with dirt-stained clothes ran with a stick and wheel from around the corner of the home. The youngest of them stopped when she noticed Doug's car. The little girl stared at him as he passed. Her blonde hair was matted with more tangles than a bird nest and Doug even saw leaves and sticks intertwined in it. The two boys, who must've been her older brothers, stopped and looked at Doug. Their faces were caked with dirt and their heads were shaved down to the scalp to likely protect against lice. Doug smiled and offered a wave. The kids didn't return the gesture but only glared at him as he passed.

Doug craned his head and chuckled.

He drove for another few minutes without seeing anyone else. In the distance he noticed a mailbox with the numbers 1313 on it. It leaned too far to one side and all it would take was a stiff breeze to blow it over. A gravel road rested next to it. Doug checked his paperwork to verify the address.

"1313 Maw Die Road. That's the one." He said as he turned down the radio. The road transitioned from dirt to gravel as his tires crunched over the rock. The road descended a little ways before a blue, single story home came into view. A large pond with a dock and gazebo sat to the right of the house. Glass bottles were fixed on the branches of small trees in the front yard. Doug pulled in behind a yellow Volkswagen Beetle. Windchimes and dreamcatchers were scattered about the porch. Various sorts of flowers and rose bushes lined the perimeter of the home. Multicolored stones were placed here and there. Two cats scurried off the porch when he shifted to park.

Doug grabbed his briefcase and exited the Impala. The abundance of windchimes was unsettling for a moment. Something about this place was giving him the willies. It was like the air was heavier here or something. He could feel it pressing down upon his shoulders. He also had the feeling of being watched. He stood next to his car and took in his surroundings. Satisfied there were no prying eyes, he made his way to the front door.

Doug adjusted his tie and cleared his throat. As he was inches from knocking on the door, it opened. The suddenness of it gave him a start. He stepped back and watched as Eileen Fuller came into view. An aroma of burning herbs filled his senses. Eileen was a petite lady, and the hump on her back made her appear even smaller. She smiled to reveal a plethora of missing teeth. The teeth she did manage to have looked rotten. The wart on the tip of her nose had a hair in it and the sight almost made Doug gag.

As if her appearance wasn't bad enough, her raspy, cadaver-like voice sent chills down Doug's spine. He gulped and eyed her carefully as she said, "Why hello there. You must be the cookware salesman. Mr. Clemmons is it? Or should I just call you Doug?"

"Doug is fine." He said though he couldn't recall telling her his last name.

"Well step inside and have a seat. Would you care for a cup of coffee, dear? It's fresh. I ground the beans this morning."

"If it's not too much trouble. That would be great. Thank you."

"No problem at all. You have a seat there, and I'll fetch the coffee."

He watched her waddle towards the kitchen. Her colorful dress almost dragged the ground behind her. He stood there with his briefcase and studied the home for a moment. He found the source of the strong aroma. A bundle of what must've been sage rested on an end table with the end smoldering over a glass bowl. Rocks and crystals were scattered everywhere he looked. He crossed to the couch with its floral pattern and sat down. He moved some crystals and figurines to make room for his briefcase. As he prepared his presentation, he heard Eileen coming back from the kitchen. She was carrying a metal tray and the saucers and mugs rattled loudly.

"Here. Let me help you with that."

Doug stood to assist, but she swatted him away.

"I may look old and feeble, but I can get around better than you think." She said as she sat the tray down next to his briefcase. "There's cream and sugar there if you like."

"Thank you, ma'am."

Doug took a cup and added some cream.

He had second thoughts of drinking the coffee as something about all of this reminded him of Hansel and Gretel. He fought to hold back the grin trying to spread across his face. He sipped the coffee, and a searing pain caused him to grimace when the hot liquid touched his tongue. It was like sticking his tongue into a flame.

"What's the matter my dear?" Eileen asked as she held her mug up about to take a drink herself.

Doug shook his head and grit his teeth.

"You have a bad tooth or something?"

"No. It's these damn bumps on my tongue. Pardon my language ma'am."

"No need for apology. I've heard worse. May I see?"

"Oh, it's nothing."

"You sure didn't act like it was nothing. Come here and let me look."

Feeling like a kid showing his grandma his new boo boo, Doug rose from the couch and bent at the waste in front of Eileen. He stuck out his tongue and let her look.

He watched a crooked grin slowly appear. She began to chuckle.

"Yup. You're a liar alright. That there's proof enough."

He repulsed from her as if slapped across the face.

"Do what?"

She looked away and took up her coffee again. "I said you're a liar. Those are lie bumps. Shouldn't be all that surprising considering your profession and all."

Doug stood there with his hands to his hips, searching for a comeback.

"Oh, sit down. Don't get your panties all bunched up."

"Lady, I'm not going to stand here and take these insults. Now, if you'll excuse me, I'm going to gather my things and be on my way."

"Suit yourself. Those bumps won't get any better though. Not without the property remedy. You've done said one too many lies for them just to disappear on their own."

"You're crazy. You know that?" Doug said as he shut his briefcase and clamped the latches. He angled for the door and said, "Thank you for the coffee."

"I can make those bumps go away." The old lady said as he was stepping through the door frame.

Doug paused and stood there with his back to her.

"It'll be like they were never there in the first place."

He turned around to face her.

"Yeah? How's that?"

"Come here and I'll show you."

He breathed deep and studied her for a moment. Giving in, he sat his briefcase down and shut the door.

"That's the spirit. Now, if it's to work, you have to do exactly as I say? Understood?"

"What are you some kind of witch?"

"Not exactly. Now sit down and listen closely."

"If you start communicating with the dead or talking about sacrifices, I'm outta here."

"Oh shut up. I've done told you I'm not a damn witch, okay?"

"Then what are you?"

"Don't worry about it. Do you want to get rid of the bumps or not?"

He narrowed his gaze and sighed.

"Very well. Do you carry a pocketknife?"

"Yeah, why?"

"We'll need it."

"For what?"

She held out her hand and tightened her lips.

He dug in his pocket and placed the knife in her hand.

"Are you left-handed or right-handed?"

"I'm a lefty why?"

"Then you'll need to take this knife and cut a line across your right palm. You'll need to follow the line that runs from the base of your pointer finger all the way down to your wrist below the meaty part of your thumb." She held up her own palm and ran a finger across the line to demonstrate.

"Are you crazy? I'm not cutting myself."

"Well, that's certainly your prerogative, but the bumps will stay until you do as I tell you. It's your choice."

He thought it over for a minute.

"What's after that?"

"I'll tell you once you complete the first step."

They held each other's gaze.

Doug scooted to the edge of his seat and unfolded the blade. He held out his right palm and sank the tip of the knife at the beginning of the line below his pointer as she had said. He squinted and scrunched his nose as he drug the blade across his palm. Blood began to ooze. He reached the bottom of his palm and let out a quick breath. "Now what?"

"Sit the knife down. Take your left hand and rub it in the blood. Then cross your left index and middle fingers thirty times. Each time you do so, say *truth for lies. Truth for lies.* Do it now."

He followed her orders.

After the thirtieth time, he looked up at her and asked, "Now what?"

"Now, you don't lie for thirty days. You should notice the bumps going away by tonight. But remember, you cannot lie for thirty days. It's an oath."

"What happens if I do?"

"You don't want to know."

A FEW WEEKS had passed and true to her word, the bumps on Doug's tongue had disappeared by the time he was ready for bed that night. He has been careful ever since not to fib. However, he may have backslidden this morning. He was meeting with an older couple who reminded him a lot of Frank and Bertha. The wife decided she liked the display cookware and like Bertha, the lady asked if she could save a few bucks on shipping by taking the display. Doug chose his words carefully and it wasn't until he was almost out the door that the old lady began her bombardment of questions. He eventually caved into his carnal ways and told a little white lie. It wasn't a big lie, but it was a lie none the less. Sweat beads broke out on his forehead and he felt a lump form in his throat. The lady had the answers she wanted, and Doug was out the door. He checked his tongue in the mirror as soon as he shut the car door. Nothing had happened.

Yet.

By the time the sun had set, he had that familiar pain flash across his tongue when he took his first bite of supper at the diner. The meatloaf looked so savory and had his mouth watering the second he spotted it on the menu. He'd ordered a side of green beans and mashed potatoes to go with it. Except for a lonely looking old man in overalls and a young courting couple, Doug was the only customer. He cursed when the meatloaf hit his tastebuds. He shut his eyes and wiggled his tongue behind his teeth. A moment later the waitress came over and asked if everything was alright. He told her it was and almost lied to say it was a toothache but caught himself and said he would be okay.

The waitress went into a long story about getting her wisdom teeth removed once and how the dentist had messed her jaw up in the process.

Said her jaw clicked for three years after the surgery and it felt like an evil fairy was chiseling on bone every time she chewed or talked.

Doug glared up at her.

"Can I get you anything?"

"I'm good, thanks."

She left and vanished into the kitchen.

Doug looked around the diner at the other customers. They dropped their heads and went back to what they were doing.

Doug stuck his tongue out and felt it with his finger and thumb.

"Dear God." He mumbled.

How had he not felt the huge knot on his tongue? It was five times larger than before. Now that it had been brought to his attention, he could feel it throbbing up against his bottom row of teeth. It had a pulse and with each pump it sent a shockwave of pain. Doug breathed deep and steadied himself. He went back to his meal and was sure to chew on the opposite side. It still hurt like the devil, but his empty stomach pushed him onward.

He finished his supper and left three dollars on the table which would be enough for a about a dollar tip he supposed. He made it back to his car and drove to the motel in Georgetown.

Once there, he tossed his briefcase on the bed and locked the door. He then marched to the bathroom, flicked on the light, and shoved his face in the mirror. He stretched out his tongue and looked in horror as the pulsing bump had grown even larger just since he left the diner. It had spread to cover the entire right front corner of his tongue. It was a feverish red again with a white center to it. He grinded his molars and growled before searching for something to pop it with. He combed through all the drawers, checked the cabinet behind the mirror, but all he could find was a pair of scissors. His heart skipped a beat at the thought of using them.

He cursed aloud. His words were garbled. He cursed again, "I can't eve tock right."

He went back to the bed where his suitcase rested. He dug through it for several minutes before finally coming up with a safety pin tucked away in a side pocket. He went back to the mirror and retrieved his lighter. He held the needle over the flame until it was red. Doug swallowed hard as he took turns looking at the needle and his growing tongue. He smacked his cheek and beat his chest in an effort to gain the courage. He leaned into the mirror and sank the needle into the bulging bump, half expecting it to explode on impact. It didn't. He screamed in agony and forced himself to dig into it, hoping he could dig out the worm like you would a white head. It wasn't working. Blood trickled out and he spit into the sink. The throbbing pain was excruciating. He sat the needle down and placed both hands on the counter. He scratched his cheek and looked down at the pair of scissors on the sink.

"No. Top it Doog."

The scissors were pulling his hand like a magnet. Before he had time to think it over, he had gripped the scissors with his left hand and was pulling out his tongue with his right. It reminded him of a man about to chop the head off a snapping turtle for stew. He'd watched his grandpa and uncles do it before. They'd take hold of the head, stretch it on a log, and whack it right off. His tongue began to writhe as he felt the muscle squirm with anticipation of what was coming. He brought the scissors up to his mouth. He began to moan as he squinted his eyes. Just as he was guiding the tip of his tongue in between the blades, a sharp hiss filled the room. In his horror, he saw something in the mirror that sent a shock jolting through his body. His tongue had split into two and slithered out to touch the mirror. A dark shadow passed behind his shoulder. Doug slammed his eyes shut, ceased up, and squeezed the scissors.

He heard something plop into the sink. He felt warm liquid flood his mouth. He couldn't taste anything, but he could sure feel everything. He screamed again and flashed open his eyes. He looked down to find a squirming piece of bloody tongue wriggling in the sink. It reminded him of a snake with its head chopped off.

"Oh, me Gawd." He somehow managed.

He looked in the mirror. He was a mess. Blood was gushing down his neck and soaking his shirt and blazer. He cursed and grabbed a towel.

His mind flashed to the first aid kit he kept in his car. With the whole corner of a towel stuffed in his mouth, he raced outside and grabbed the first aid kit beneath the passenger seat.

An older fellow with a bear gut and long beard stopped from climbing into his truck to see what all the fuss was about.

"You okay mister?"

Doug looked up with the towel still stuffed in his mouth and waved the man off.

"Suit yourself, you crazy bastard." The old man said before getting into his truck.

Doug rushed back inside with the kit and flung it open. Tape and band aids went flying across the bed. Doug found the gauze and began unrolling it. He took it back to the bathroom and proceeded to wrap his tongue with it until it looked like a nub from a bombing victim. It was so big he couldn't close his mouth all the way.

Gasping for breath, he stepped out of the bathroom and fell on the corner of the bed. He ran a hand through his hair and scratched his head. One thought shouted in the forefront of his mind. He had to go see Eileen. She would know what to do.

A little over an hour later, Doug found himself turning down her gravel road. It was just after nine o'clock when he knocked on her door. The property was dark, and he feared she had already turned in for the night. He had a sudden vision of her stepping out and clutching a double barrel shotgun.

"Ilean. It's me, Doog. I ned you helt." He added as he continued to knock.

"I'm coming."

He heard her patter across the hardwood floor. He stepped back from the door and watched it open.

A crooked grin stretched her wrinkled face.

He furrowed his brows at her and said with a mumble, "What so funny?"

"I knew you would be back."

She waved him inside and motioned towards the couch, "Sit right there, I'll be back."

He did as he was told and waited for her. He could feel a pulse in his tongue as it throbbed with each beat. Nausea began to form as he fought back the pain.

He heard Eileen coming down the hall.

She carried a granite bowl and pestle in one hand and a bunch of herbs and flowers in the other. She had a roll of gauze tape tucked under her arm.

"What's zat?"

"Don't worry about it. How much did you cut off?"

Doug held out his thumb and forefinger, keeping them about three inches apart.

"That much, huh?"

He nodded.

"Did you see the serpents tongue?"

He got quiet and only looked at her. He felt his heart knock hard at the thought of what happened at the motel. He swallowed hard.

"I take that as a yes. What about a shadow? Did you see any shadows?"

He nodded slowly.

Eileen sighed and shook her head.

"I told you not to lie for thirty days. You asked what would happen if you did...well now you know."

Eileen placed some herbs and flower petals into the bowl and began to grind them into a paste with the pestle. She spent a good ten minutes or so mashing everything together.

When she was finished, she sat the bowl aside and looked up at Doug.

"You can take the bandage off now."

He blinked.

"Go on. I'll give you a new one."

He huffed out a breath and began to unravel it. He grimaced as it got closer to the end.

Eileen whistled and said, "My word, you really did a number on that thing didn't you? What did you use, a pair of shears? Goodness gracious."

"Just git on wit it."

"Well alright then. It might hurt a little at first, but you'll heal pretty quick. That is, as long as you don't tell anymore lies." She lowered her chin at him and raised her brows.

He shook his head and said, "No mo."

She chuckled.

She balled up the herb paste and told him to stick his tongue out. He did and she plopped the paste where the missing meat was. He jerked back and yelped.

"Easy now. Keep your tongue out so I can wrap it."

Tears were running down his cheeks.

She finished with the gauze and sat back in her recliner.

"There. All finished. See I told you it wouldn't hurt for long. My guess is you'll be all healed up in a few days. But remember what I said, no lying. Right?"

He nodded.

"What are you looking at me like that for?" She asked him.

He held out his hands, palms up as if asking for an explanation.

"Look. I don't understand it all myself, but I know it's real, okay? You ever read the Bible, Doug?"

He shrugged his shoulders, "A little."

"Well, it talks about the devil being the father of lies. Hell, it was his lie to Eve that led to the original sin. All throughout the scripture you'll find places where it associates the devil with lying. My guess is he must be attracted to those who lie. I mean we all do it, but I think some more than others. I think those bumps are a warning of sorts. It's like they're saying 'hey, you better watch yourself. You've been doing an awful lot of lying lately, may want to tone it down.' You see what happens when you ignore the warning?"

He nodded with wide eyes.

"That's all I'll say about that. You go and get back to wherever it is you came from. I don't want to see you anymore unless you have a free set of cookware, you hear?"

They shared a small laugh.

Doug stood and crossed for the door.

He turned and looked at Eileen as she stood behind him.

"Tank you." He said and hugged her.

Doug got into his car and aimed for Georgetown. He promised aloud that he'd never lie again. Something deep within wondered if that was a lie in and of itself. He gulped at the thought of anything worse than what he'd just experienced.

He wondered if part of his tongue was still wiggling in the sink back at the motel. The thought sent a chill down the back of his neck. *Truth over lies. Truth over lies. Truth over lies.* He repeated the words as he traveled along the lonely interstate.

The Vanishing of Thomas Marvin

I started working for the old man back in the summer of 1992. He lived down the hill from us and was only a short bike ride from my house. I had turned thirteen that spring and was thinking of starting a grass cutting business that summer. That was before Thomas Marvin offered me good pay to help him and his wife tend to things around their house. They were both in their early eighties and were having trouble doing the things they used to. I talked to my parents about the old man's offer. They both thought it'd be wise to take the old man up on the job. That simple decision has forever changed my life.

Thomas Marvin owned over one hundred and sixty acres with fifty-three of it being old tobacco fields. He and his wife, Gloria, had made their living for forty years harvesting tobacco in those fields. Together they ran a company which at one point employed about a dozen or more people. The old man was smart with his money and had invested wisely through the years. He understood the pros and cons of debt and interest and learned to use them both in his favor. He respected every penny that was made and was always sure to put it to good use. When he and Gloria retired from the Tobacco business, they leased eighty acres of his land to a local hunting club. The back portion of the land was a mixture of wetlands and hardy pines, which made it perfect hunting grounds. The land was plentiful with ducks, hogs, deer, and bear. The hunting club was happy to pay a premium for the prized land. At one point, they even offered a seven-figure deal to buy it from him outright. The old man refused the offer.

I learned a lot from the old man for the four years I worked for him. He was always telling me tips and secrets about money and investing. Half of the time his words were gibberish as I had trouble understanding his train of thought. As I've gotten older, I've realized just how smart the old rascal really was.

The first summer I worked for him he paid me three bucks an hour plus an extra twenty a week if I read him an hour of the Wall Street Journal each morning. At first, I thought any man who wanted to read or listen to an hour of the Wall Street Journal had to have one foot in the insane asylum, but the more I read of it the less I came to loathe it. After the first month of reading to him for an hour each morning, I actually began understanding some of the things it was talking about. Of course, Tom explained a lot of things along the way. He was Tom to me. He always stressed I just call him Tom. He didn't like for me to call him Mr. Marvin or Thomas. Gloria could call him Thomas, but not me. Tom was what he preferred.

Summer came and went in a flash. My parents were happy I'd found something I enjoyed doing and was able to make some decent money doing it. The way we all figured, another two summers like the first and I could buy my first car soon after I got my license.

The summer of '93 rolled around, and Tom bumped my pay to $3.50 an hour plus an extra $25 a week for reading the Journal to him each morning. He even offered a hundred-dollar bonus at the end of the summer if I helped him finish painting his barn and repair a few slats in his privacy fence beside Pam Rogers, their neighbor.

It was a few weeks before I went back to school for the fall when Tom mentioned the idea he had of buying a few milk cows to graze in a section of the old tobacco field. He planned to till up the dead plants with his tractor and throw down some grass seed in hopes of making about a two-acre pasture for the cows. He even had plans to build a new barn. He said Gloria had grown up on a farm and had always wanted cows and chickens and such. The way he figured, with the price of milk and eggs the way it was, sounded like a good opportunity to please the wife and save a few bucks while he's at it. I remember he snickered and elbowed me in the ribs when he told me that.

"The way I see it kid, you'll have more work than you know what to do with next summer. If you'll help a feller out with it, I'll be willing to bump ya pay to four an hour plus thirty a week for reading the Journal to me. What'd ya say? Sound square enough for ya?" He said with an outstretched hand.

I didn't even have to think about it. I nodded and shook his hand faster than a rabbit on crack.

It was when he got the cows that things started getting weird. Me, a few of my buddies from school, and an older colored man whom Tom had known since the army, built the barn and redid a section of his tobacco field early that summer. Once we were finished, Tom went to a cattle auction somewhere down in Chester, South Carolina and bought four milk cows. He had them delivered the next day. Gloria had named them Betsy, Bertha, Brenda, and Bonnie. Why they all had to start with a B I never did understand, but that was their names. I remember Charles, the old colored man, laughed and laughed when he heard Gloria rattle off each of the names.

"You folk crack me up. I kid you not." He'd said.

A few weeks after they got the cows, we received a phone call from Tom around two in the morning. My dad was the one who answered it as all we had back then was a landline. I heard him fumble his way into the kitchen, flick the light on, and lift the phone out of its cradle. My dad's voice was thick with gravel, and I could just picture him standing there shirtless in his boxers, rubbing his eyes trying to figure out who in the world was calling at two in the morning.

"You said what now? People are in your field? Who is this?"

By then I had crawled out of bed and was coming down the hall.

"Who? Thomas? Thomas Marvin?"

I entered the kitchen the same time my mother did. She stood in the arch of the hallway tying a knot in her robe. She squinted at my dad and mouthed, *What's wrong?*

Dad shrugged his shoulders.

"Well, what are they doing? What? How many are they? Jesus..."

His voice trailed off. I could hear a voice on the other end but couldn't make out the words. I heard a pop sound and saw my dad flinch before pulling the phone from his ear and staring at it for a short moment.

"What was that?" I asked him.

"It sounded like a gunshot," then into the phone, "Thomas are you alright? Hey. What's going on? Can you hear me?"

I heard two more shots before his voice came back.

I watched as my dad stood there listening and making odd faces.

"Have you called the cops?"

Mom said, "Is he okay? What's going on over there?"

My dad shook his head and held up a hand.

"Yeah. Okay. Well, they shouldn't bother you no more. It sounds like it was probably some teenagers just messing with ya. Me and Derrick will come by tomorrow to check on things with ya. Alright. You be careful now. We'll see ya tomorrow. Alright. Bye."

"Is everything alright? What's going on?" My mom asked as I was about to do the same.

Dad looked at the floor, sighed, and shook his head.

"Lord have mercy. That old fart is losing his mind."

"What is it?"

"He said they were a bunch of lights down in his field where the cows are at. Said he heard them mooing and causing a stir. He got up and said he heard a bunch of voices and saw lights flickering on and off. Said everything disappeared when he fired his shotgun in the air. Tried saying he saw lights in the trees and stuff too." Dad looked at me and said, "Has he ever talked that strange around you before?"

"No. I've never heard him talk like that. Something had to get him stirred up."

"Hmph. I told him we'd come by tomorrow to help him look around. Said he didn't want to call the sheriff. Said he just wanted us to know in case they tried fooling around up here."

Mama added, "That's awfully odd for him to call like that. I hope he's not coming down with dementia or nothing. I know Gloria had told me the other week about how forgetful he's becoming."

"Oh lord. Don't say that." Dad said.

We went back to bed and the next morning, which happened to be a Saturday, my mama cooked a good breakfast of liver mush and eggs before we all headed over to Tom and Gloria's.

We tried knocking on the front door which was opened except for the screen storm door. After not getting an answer, my mama opened the door and poked her head inside. She called out for them, but there was never a returning voice.

I said, "I bet he's in his field."

"He's probably right. C'mon honey, let's look around back," Dad said.

Mama stepped off the porch and joined me and Dad as we rounded the corner of the house. Off in the distance near the back corner of Tom's field, I noticed two people standing there. I could barely make them out, but him and Gloria were looking at something on the ground. There were two large, black mounds resting before them.

"Hank, is that what I think it is?" My mama asked.

Dad grunted and squinted his eyes. He shielded the sun with his hand. He grumbled a curse under his breath.

"Who would do such a thing? Are they dead Hank? I hope they're not dead."

Dad shook his head and said, "I don't know, but those cows sure ain't moving."

As we drew closer, Tom and Gloria spotted us. Tom was holding his straw hat in his hand and waved it in the air when he saw us. Gloria stood next to him with her arms crossed. She wore a long, khaki skirt and a baby blue blouse. Her silver hair was tied into a tight bun.

Tom had his hands to his hips and studied the sight before him. He tightened his lips and peeked up at us as we approached.

"What in the hell happened, Tom?" Dad asked.

The old man shook his head, "I knew I should've came down here to check on em last night. Gloria was afraid one of them people would get me. I told her I liked my chances with the scatter gun." He paused and sighed before adding, "I ain't never seen nothing like this before. I've grown up around cattle most of my life, and I've seen what happens when a coyote or big cat gets ahold of one of them. But this..." His words trailed off as he pointed down at the cow's face.

We were standing behind the animal and couldn't see the face or belly all that good. When we stepped around to see what Tom was talking about, I remember feeling like my heart had taken a shock from a cattle prod. The majority of the flesh around Brenda's face had been stripped away to leave a bloody, grinning skull. I could see her tongue had been cut in half. Her eyes bulged like two ping pong balls. Scanning down the body, I saw her gut had a round hole which had been sliced with prefect precision. Her udder was missing, and her blue, gray intestines lay spewed on the ground. A pungent odor hung in the air. Despite the gore, I couldn't see a drop of blood anywhere.

My mama gasped and covered her mouth before turning away.

"Jesus. What the hell?" Dad said as he scrunched his face at the sight and looked to Tom for answers.

Tom shook his head and pointed his hat to the other cow lying lifeless about ten yards from us.

"Bonnie's the same way. I had to lock Betsy and Bertha in the barn. They kept hanging around and nudging 'em. Those poor things moaned and groaned like people grieving at funeral or somfin."

Gloria sniffled and said, "I told Tom I want to get some cameras set up so we can catch whoever did this. These poor cows didn't deserve this. People are evil nowadays."

Mama came back to us and added, "You need to call the Sheriff so they can file a report."

Tom tightened his lips and grunted, "Sheriff will just laugh at us. That sorry rascal will try saying a bear did it or somfin. Gloria's right, we need camera's so we can have proof of who's messing around."

"Me and Derrick can help you put them up." Dad said.

Tom looked at me and Dad and said, "Really? I'd appreciate that. I don't know the first thing about today's technology."

A few days later, after Tom used his tractor to bury Brenda and Bonnie, me and Dad helped set the cameras up for him. My mom found an eight-camera system at RadioShack that came with the DVR box and monitor. It took us about two hours one evening to get it all set up, but it was worth it. We placed the monitor on a desk next to the living room so the two of them could keep a check on it as they watched their nightly TV shows. We had four cameras stationed at each corner of the house with the other four pointing towards the field, barn, and tool shed.

As much as we thought we were helping at the time, I think those cameras may have been a mistake because that was when the old man's paranoia really began. His late-night calls became a weekly routine after that. He'd call swearing up and down somebody was messing around his house. He'd call cussing up a storm saying he saw lights on the camera and heard people in his field. We'd go over there the next day to run the cameras back but could never find anything more than dust orbs or bugs floating by.

That summer ended without further incident, and I went back to school to start my sophomore year at Clover High. Kids at school had somehow heard about the deaths of Tom's two cows and boy did the rumors spread. My buddies would often greet me in the hallway wearing hats covered in tinfoil. I heard whispers about everything from aliens, the CIA, Bigfoot, a satanic cult, you name it. How people found out about those cows, I never understood. I guess that's the works of living in a small town though. I sometimes wondered if maybe the culprits even attended my school.

I went back to work that summer, and after only a week on Tom's farm, I found Gloria lying in the field, naked, and lifeless. It was at dawn and Tom had driven into town to gather supplies for another fence we were to build. Gloria had fixed breakfast as always and the two enjoyed a meal together before starting the day. Her official cause of death was ruled a heart attack, and despite her nakedness, there was no indication of foul play. As strange as it all was, it looked like she had simply stepped out of the shower and walked into the field before her heart gave out. The bathroom mirror was still damp with moisture and water droplets led from the shower to the back deck. A bath towel was found twenty feet from her body. It appeared something had drawn her out to the field. But what? Had she heard something? When the camera footage was rolled back, it was nothing but gray and white static for two hours surrounding the time it all happened. Still to this day, no one has ever learned the truth behind Gloria's death.

The tragic event only added to Tom's already fragile mental state. The man became a recluse after her death. My parents and I did our best to be there for him, but his behavior became creepy and unpredictable. He talked nonstop about people wandering in his field at night, seeing strange lights again, and hearing voices calling to him late into the night.

I will never forget the night he called and said the people were in his home.

My dad had answered the phone again and was on the brink of cursing. I watched as he gritted his teeth at the annoyance that Tom's midnight calls had become. His anger dissipated quick, and I knew by the look on his face something was wrong. He got real quiet and let the old man talk.

"What is it this time?" Mom asked in a mid yawn.

I watched Dad swallow hard before saying, "Helen, get my pistol from my nightstand and grab my coat."

She squinted her eyes.

"Please. Just do it."

Mom went to their bedroom and came back with the items in hand. She handed dad his coat and he slid into it while still listening to Tom with the phone cradled on his shoulder. He took his .357 revolver, checked the cylinder, then stuffed it into his coat pocket.

"Tom, stay put. I'll be right there."

The phone jingled in its cradle.

He turned to us and wiped the sleep from his face.

"What's going on?" I asked.

"Tom said four people were just in his house. One of them he claimed was Gloria."

"What?" My mom asked in a hoarse whisper.

Dad nodded, "Said it was a big man, a woman, Gloria, and some little girl. Said they came in the front door while he was watching TV and started roaming through his house like they were looking for something."

"Oh my God. Do you want me to call the police?"

Dad shook his head, "No, not yet. It kind of sounded like he had been drinking a bit, so I'm hoping he's just high on the sauce. I'm going to go check on him to be sure."

"You're not going down there by yourself."

Dad ran a hand through his thick hair and sighed, "Well, c'mon. But grab my .38 so you can keep it in the truck with you and Derrick."

Minutes later we were pulling into Tom's driveway. Dad parked the truck and scanned our surroundings. He rolled the windows down and listened. The air felt different here. It had an electric charge to it or something. Like the way it feels during a summer storm just before a lightning strike. It was almost difficult to breathe. I could feel something pressing down on me. It was like the pressure was higher than normal. The night was quiet except for a soft breeze lofting through the trees.

"Alright. Stay here. You see anything odd you blow the horn. Got it?"

Mama nodded.

"Anybody approaches you . . . well that's why you have the .38, right?"

She nodded again and said, "Are you sure we shouldn't call the police, honey?"

"Not yet. Let me have a look around first."

He climbed out of the truck and shut the door. Leaning in through the window he said, "Lock the doors and roll the windows up."

As Dad was finishing his words, the flood light to Tom's back porch came on. We each jerked our attention in time to see Tom, butt naked, walking down the steps of his porch and heading for the field.

Dad cursed and called after him, "Tom! Tom, what the hell are you doing?"

Tom didn't acknowledge him but kept striding to the field.

"Wait here." Dad said before going after him.

We kept the windows down, so I stood up in the cab to lean out and look at them. I watched Dad reach Tom and place his own coat around him. Tom jerked away and said, "Leave me alone. I'm going to see Gloria."

Dad stepped back from him and stared. He tried again to put the coat on him. Tom spun around and back handed my dad across the face. Dad blinked in disbelief. I watched him grit his teeth after rubbing his jaw.

"Hey. Tom, listen to me." Dad said as he took hold of Tom's arm.

Dad shook his shoulders and patted Tom's cheek to wake him from what had to be a dream.

Tom stared at him for a long time before suddenly snapping back to reality. He shook his head and began looking around in a panic.

Dad closed the coat around him, and Tom blushed as he realized his nakedness. He turned and looked at me and Mom with a face of shame and horror. He turned back to Dad, and I heard him say, "What happened? Hank, what happened?"

Dad put his arm around him and soothed him.

"I think you had a little too much to drink, Tom. It's alright. You're fine. C'mon, let's get you back inside, okay?"

"I heard Gloria. I heard her calling for me from the field. I heard her plain as day. She was down there, Hank. I know she was. You have to check. You have to go see."

Dad looked at me and Mama and make a *God help us* face.

"I'll check, Tom. You need to go inside and get to bed."

"I saw those lights right after I saw those people. Those lights were back in the field, and I heard Gloria down there calling for help."

"Tom, I'll look around the house for you before I go to be sure no one's in the field, alright."

"It's not so much the people I'm worried about."

I remember that statement struck me as odd. I have never forgotten the way he said that.

I watched Dad take Tom back inside as he rambled the whole way about the lights and hearing strange noises and such.

After Dad got Tom situated, he came back out, and we rode down into the field to have a look around.

The electric charge I felt in his driveway had multiplied ten-fold when we reached the field. So much so that I could literally feel the hairs on my arms raising as if being pulled by a magnetic force. It reminded me of standing close to a television set and feeling the static charge it gives.

"Do y'all feel that?"

"Feel what?" Mama asked me.

"You don't feel anything?"

She shook her head.

"Dad, do you feel it?"

He thought for a moment, "No. What are you talking about?"

The headlights blinked out when he finished his words.

Mama yelped. I leaned into her and squeezed her arm. Dad cursed and slapped the steering wheel. It wasn't just the lights that went out, the whole truck had died.

I remember how silent everything was. There were no crickets, tree frogs, or cicadas. The field was washed in an eerie stillness. I could literally hear my mama's heartbeat.

The night was overcast and hid the moon. The field was nothing but a black abyss. It was like we had driven into a starless space. A galaxy void of life and light. I swallowed the knot in my throat. My heart pounded against my ribs. My skin crawled as gooseflesh rifled over my entire body.

Dad turned the key and the truck sputtered then made a clicking sound.

"Damn it!"

He tried again but got the same result.

He sat back in his seat with a huff and rested his chin in the cradle of his hand as he stared out the driver's window.

"Do you have your jumper box with you?" Mama asked.

"No, it's in the garage. I forgot to put it back in here after I had to jump the boat battery off the other day."

"Oh my God, Hank. How could you forget to put it back?"

"I just did, alright? Let's give it a few minutes, and I'll try it again."

Those few minutes felt like a few hours as they crept along at the rate of an out-of-date gas pump.

"Do you hear that?" Mama asked as she craned her head.

I didn't hear it at first, but after about ten seconds of listening, I began to hear it too. It was a high-pitched whistle calling from the tree line. Sounded like a high frequency dog training device.

"What in the hell is that?" Dad said as he squinted and grimaced.

The sound was ear piercing and forced us to cover our ears.

Mama began slapping Dad's leg to get him to try the ignition again. He did. The truck fired right up like nothing had ever happened. He threw it into gear and spun grass and dirt to get us out of there. He made a quick stop back at Tom's house to be sure the old man was alright. He raced in and raced out. Said he was asleep in his boxers on the couch.

Nothing else happened the rest of the summer. I went on to help him around the house like I always did. I was making good money by then and was doing good to save for the truck I'd been wanting. It wasn't until the third week of helping him the next summer that things got even stranger.

The big project that summer was going to be a new and bigger chicken coop. Tom had ordered all the material and had it delivered. Me, Dad, and Charles were to build it over the weekend when they were off work. Me and Dad drove over to Tom's a little before seven that Saturday morning. Thursday was the last time we'd talked to him. We got out of the truck and made it onto the front porch. Dad opened the screened door and gave a few good knocks on the window of the main door. He stepped back and sipped on his coffee thermos. How anybody could drink that nasty stuff is beyond me. Maybe one day I'll grow to like it, but I don't know. My tastebuds have an awful lot of growing to do before that day ever comes. We waited there on the porch, but never heard any movement. He'd told dad on Thursday for us to have breakfast with him before we got started. Said he'd have sausage and egg biscuits ready for us.

"The old rascal probably forgot what he told me about those biscuits." Dad said with a grin.

"It wouldn't surprise me." I said as I chuckled and leaned into the window to peer towards the living room. I could see the TV showing a rerun of his favorite show, *Gunsmoke.* I smiled and scanned the rest of the room.

What in the world?

I could see the side of his recliner. There were clothes laid out like someone was sitting there but they had no form to fill them.

I pulled back and looked at Dad.

"Dad, c'mere and have a look at this."

"What now?"

Together we looked in, cupping our hands around the glass.

Dad wrinkled his brow and didn't say anything. He stepped back and went to the door. He tried the handle. It opened without protest. He gave me an odd look before we made our way inside.

"Tom, you up buddy?" He called out.

"Tom?" I added.

Dad did a quick glance around the home as I went to the recliner for a better look.

A shirt, pants, underwear, and socks were all laid out on the recliner like he should be sitting right there in front of me. Even his silver chained watch that he wore on his left wrist was stationed where his hand would be on the arm rest.

I gulped and called for Dad.

"He's not here." He said as he strode up beside me.

I pointed to the watch.

"What in the hell?"

About that time, we heard a car pull into the driveway. I turned and looked out the window to find Charles's truck parking behind ours.

The three of us went on to search the house again before driving down into the field. We never found Tom Marvin that day. The police were called to investigate. They spent the next few days combing over every inch of the property, using search dogs and the whole nine yards. The DNR did a thorough sweep of the woods to be sure he hadn't wandered off anywhere. The only evidence that was ever discovered were his clothes laid out on the recliner. It looked like he had been sitting there watching *Gunsmoke* and simply evaporated out of the room.

He was ruled a missing person and his picture was stapled to every light pole and store window in town. Multiple op eds were printed in the town paper. A handful of independent journalists came to town to investigate once word began to spread of the strange circumstances. More than once, they came to our house for questioning. We never gave them the time of day. Mama and Dad said they'd likely spin things how they needed to suit their story anyway.

With Tom and Gloria never having kids or much other family, the home and all of his assets went into probate. We were able to gain authority to sell Betsy and Bertha to a good home where they could be properly cared for. We did our best to keep his place up, by cutting the grass and keeping the weeds from overgrowing near the house.

It wasn't until a year or so later that we received a letter in the mail from an attorney's office addressed to my name.

Mama had gotten it from the mail while I was at school, and fought every urge to open it, but waited for me and Dad to get home before discovering what it was all about.

I opened it with great suspicion as Mama and Dad watched over my shoulder.

The letter basically said that Tom and Gloria had left the home, land, and all other assets to me who they considered in their will as their adopted grandson. It had a breakdown of the different brokerage accounts they shared together, as well as the amount of gold and silver stored in a safe deposit box at his bank in town. The sum of the estate was worth over $2.2 million. The letter said there would be instructions from Tom within the safe deposit box as to how best preserve and protect the wealth.

Mama dropped the glass she was drinking from, and it shattered on the floor.

Dad stepped away and held a hand to his head, breathing deeply.

Tom was never found, and the majority of the money he left behind for me was left where he had it. Except for $750,000. Five hundred of it was used to start a construction and real estate business which, Dad, Mama and me began operating after I graduated high school. I went on to earn an associate's degree in finance from the local community college.

I followed Tom's instructions to the T. Except for the other $250,000 which I used to create a non-profit investigative entity to look into other strange stories such as Tom's. I bought a thirty-three-foot RV and loaded it down with all of today's best technology to help discover the truth behind the unexplained events around the country. For about three months out of the year, the three of us are on the road researching different stories which have been submitted to our website. We have investigated everything from aliens, Bigfoot, cattle mutilations, missing people, you name it. We've been doing it now for about thirty years, I guess. I even have drones and FLIR technology to scan the woods and stuff. It's a fun and adventurous gig as you never know what might come through the inbox. I feel that it's a way for us to remember Tom by helping to solve the mysteries of others.

I think it's something he'd be proud of.

At least, I hope so.

Dead Awake

Savannah Bird was a jovial twenty-year-old who was a psychology major in her third year of study at LSU. For spring break, she, her boyfriend Jake, and a handful of their closest friends went to New Orleans for the week. On the third night around two in the morning the crew had just left a bar and was heading back to the hotel when Savannah stumbled into a vagabond begging for change on the corner of Bourbon and French Street. The old lady wore tattered clothes and cheap jewelry. Her skin was sagging, and she stunk to high heavens. Savannah apologized for the occurrence, but the old lady only glared at her with searing eyes. Savannah felt a chill run down her spine as she found herself locked in the woman's gaze.

The gypsy looking woman held out a cup of loose change and rattled it at Savannah. The old lady scowled at her again when Savannah shook her head.

Jake took Savannah's hand and turned to usher her away, but the old lady seized Savannah's arm and yanked her from Jake's grip. With the suddenness of a viper's strike, the old lady plucked a grouping of hair from Savannah's scalp. She yelped and watched in shock as the old lady rubbed the hair and began to chant.

"What the hell, old lady? What's your problem?"

The lady smiled to show rotting teeth and spoke in what could have been Latin.

Jake and the others wrinkled their brows.

Savannah couldn't move. Her flesh tingled as a sizzling flash of heat flooded over her. Her cheeks flushed and she felt her pulse thump strong in her neck. Her vision blurred for a moment before she felt Jake whisk her away. She felt herself go limp as Jake and her friend, Courtney, dragged her around the block.

The old lady cackled while rubbing the hair between her fingers. Savannah watched her until she faded to black as her eyelids closed without her command.

By the time they had reached the hotel, her body was ravaged with fever. Her eyes had rolled to the back of her head, and tremors had overtaken her. A half hour later, Jake and their friends rushed her to the ER.

Savannah was declared dead within two hours.

THE FUNERAL WAS held three days later. Jake sat in the front row of the church along with

Savannah's parents and younger sister. The songs had been sung, a brief word spoken from a close friend, and now the Rabbi had just taken the stage to begin his message.

Within five minutes of the eulogy, everyone began to hear noises coming from the casket.

SHE COULD HEAR a man talking. His voice seemed to echo in the far reaches of her mind. Her vision was as black as night. The air was acrid and humid. It reminded her of the inside of a locked car during a summer day. Her body felt weak, drained, and lifeless. It took all she had to open her eyes. Her spatial awareness came into focus. Her elbows were tucked tight to her ribs and her hands were folded above her naval. She swallowed and a thick, slimy glob slithered down the back of her throat. She felt it land in the pit of her empty gut. A bout of nausea rushed her, and she jerked a hand to her mouth to ward it off. Her elbow popped when she did so. She felt the silk cloth caress her flesh. Her mind was groggy, but she was slowly beginning to awaken.

Where am I? Am I at the hospital? Why is the power out?

When she went to get up, she banged her head against the wood. Her eyes flashed wide.

Why am I in a box?

The man's voice went silent followed by a crowd of gasps and murmurs.

What kind of sick joke is this?

She pressed outward with all her might. She felt the box begin to rock.

There's more gasping and wailing.

Oh my God! It's a casket! Is this my funeral?

She began to scream as she beat against her coffin.

INSIDE THE SANCTUARY people made a wild break for the exit. The lamenters screamed and cried as they tripped over one another.

Jake jolted to his feet and backpedaled down the aisle. His eyes were locked onto the casket as it had begun to shake. The cloth skirt around the bottom of the table swayed with the rocking. The pastor had stepped from the stage and uttered prayers as he looked on in horror at what was unfolding before them.

The casket popped and creaked loudly when the door started to lift. It was soon flung open before Savannah Bird began crawling out of it. She stood in front of her casket with her hands to her sides. The pastor had fled, leaving only her boyfriend, parents, and sister in the sanctuary.

SAVANNAH BIRD'S story had made international news as soon as that night. Her parents were hounded by reporters and journalists seeking answers. They had rushed her to the hospital shortly after the initial shock had worn from seeing her crawl out of her own casket. The doctors were as baffled as the rest of them. Growing up, Savannah was raised in a strict and devout Jewish home. She strayed from her parents teaching in high school and moved out the day she turned eighteen. Due to their religion, her parents refused an autopsy or the embalming of their daughter so as not to desecrate her body. Doctors explained to her that that simple decision may have been what ultimately saved her life. The only explanation doctors were able to give her was a condition known as the Lazarus Syndrome. Named after the same Lazarus in the Bible whom Jesus had raised from the dead. Doctors described it as the spontaneous return of a normal cardiac rhythm after failed attempts at resuscitation.

Doctors monitored her at the hospital for three more days but were unable to find any sign of distress or illness in her body. She was as healthy as any twenty-year-old should be. During her hospital stay she had begged for a nice juicy, rare steak. She had never been much of a meat eater before, so her cry for a rare steak had caught the family off guard. Nevertheless, on the day she made it home from the hospital, her family planned a steak dinner. Jake and her parents ensured it was served rare just as she had requested. After saying grace, they watched as she began devouring the steak like a cavewoman. Her mother had told her to mind her manners. She grinned and apologized. She dabbed her chin with a napkin and went back to eating. This time only at a slightly slower pace.

Jake sat next to her at an angle and studied her the entire time. He sipped his glass of water as she stabbed another piece of meat. He swallowed an ice cube, and it slid awkwardly down his throat as it jabbed his esophagus.

"So, what was it like being dead?" Her younger sister, Aubrey, asked her.

Their mother scolded her for asking such a thing at the table.

"I'm sorry. I mean I'm only asking what we all want to know."

Savannah swallowed a piece of steak and said with a full cheek, "It's alright mom. She's right. I'm sure you're all wondering the same thing. Well. To tell you the truth. I don't remember. It was kind of like sleeping, I guess. I mean the last thing I remember is falling asleep on the street of New Orleans before waking up in my coffin."

Their mother covered her lips with the pads of her four fingers. She shook her head as tears slipped down her face.

Their dad cleared his throat and asked, "You don't remember dreaming or anything?"

Savannah thought for a moment then wagged her head, "No. No, I never dreamed. It was just...black."

Jake sat with his arms crossed and his chin cradled in a hand. He studied her, listening to every word she spoke, watching her every mannerism. Something about this whole thing felt off to him. He struggled to place a finger on what it was, but for the life of him he couldn't get rid of the nagging feeling that something just wasn't right. His mind kept returning to the night of her death when she had bumped into that old lady on the street. Had the lady done something to her? Put a curse on her or something? It's nuts to think that way, but it's also nuts to believe his girlfriend climbed out of the coffin by herself.

"I don't know how to explain it, but I feel so much more alive now. It's like my soul is lighter, more awake I guess for lack of a better term. It's weird. I just feel so different. But in a good way if that makes sense."

Her father reached across the table and squeezed her hand, "It makes total sense honey. Praise God you're alive."

Jake forced a fake smile and continued to observe her.

Even her eyes seemed off. Their contrast was darker. Her brown eyes were almost black it seemed. Her voice had a sandpaper-like rasp to it. He studied his thoughts as he watched her consume the raw meat. She smacked her lips and smiled at him.

He smiled back.

God, something just isn't right.

He left about an hour later to allow her time with the family. The rest of the night he couldn't get her off his mind. He replayed everything in his head until he finally fell asleep on the couch. He dreamed about her every time he drifted away. He kept rewatching from the center of the church aisle as she climbed out of the casket. He jolted awake twice through the night when he saw her gray, decomposed corpse push open the lid and walk down the aisle towards him with an outstretched hand. Her flesh hung like ribbons as dirt and sticks were matted in her hair. Dark, thick veins ran across her skin like lightning strikes. She called for him with a deep, gravelly voice that wasn't her own. Her eyes were blacker than the night sky. Her pupils shined like stars as they beamed into his soul. In his dreams, he was frozen to the floor and could only stand there as she drew near him. She began to whisper the closer she got. She seized his arm and leaned in close to his face. He awoke when she started whispering in his ear. He felt her warm breath and smelt the rancidness of her. The putrid odor turned his gut. He woke up screaming until it felt like his throat was bleeding.

The last time he woke, he checked his phone to see if she ever texted him back from when he'd said goodnight. She did. Her text read: *Love you too honey bear. Can't wait to see you tomorrow. XOXO.*

The text made his brow wrinkle. She had never called him that before. He stared at the screen for a few moments before placing his phone on the coffee table and fighting to go back to sleep. He tossed and turned most of the night but managed to avoid seeing her in his dreams.

He called her the next morning around ten but couldn't reach her. He texted her but never heard back. He thought it was odd, but figured she must be busy with family, so he didn't try her again until later in the day. Worry began to seep in the longer the day went. When night came and she still hadn't responded, he made plans to visit the next day.

That night around three in the morning he was woken to the same dream he'd had the previous night. Only this time it wasn't Savannah he saw crawl out of the coffin, but the old woman from New Orleans. Her long, gray hair stretched to her knees, and she reached for him with long, crusty fingernails that looked like claws. She whispered something in his ear, but it was in another language. She cackled when he began to scream.

That morning at nine he tried calling and texting but got no answer. It was a little after nine thirty when he pulled into the Bird family's driveway. This was Friday so he thought it was odd to find both her parents' cars at home. He figured they would be at work. Especially her dad. He owned his own real estate brokerage and hardly ever missed days at work. He rationalized that maybe they had both taken the week off to be with Savannah. That made enough sense to him. He pushed the questions to the back of his mind and made his way to the front door. He pressed the doorbell and waited.

A moment passed and no one answered. He tried the bell again.

Nothing.

He leaned into the side windowpane of the door and cupped his hands around the glass. He couldn't hear any footsteps and didn't see any movement.

What the hell?

He knocked on the glass and pressed the bell twice more.

Panic began setting in as his pulse quickened.

He pulled out his phone and dialed her number. It went straight to voicemail this time. He tried her again. Same thing.

As he was about to call 911, he heard the door click. He stepped back and watched as it swung open with a gentle beckoning. No one was there. The faint sound of old music lingered in the air. Sounded like it travelled from a vinyl record. It had that static tone to it. He swallowed and peered into the home.

"Hello?" he called.

Only the 40's music answered.

He stepped inside and scanned the home.

"Hello? It's me. Jake."

He shut the door and locked it behind himself.

The music seemed to come from somewhere upstairs.

He eased his way through the home, stealing glances this way and that as he went. As he passed the kitchen, he noticed the table was set in the dining room. Dirty plates and empty wine glasses adorned the tablecloth. He took note and continued through the house.

He reached the bottom of the spiral staircase and stared towards the loft where Savannah's bedroom was located. The music continued.

The stairs creaked with every step.

His heart thumped hard. His mouth went dry. His palms were slick with sweat. He could smell candles burning.

Jake reached the top and began creeping his way down the hall towards the music. Savannah's bedroom door was cracked open.

He slid along the wall to her room. Once there, he extended a hand and gave the door a gentle nudge.

His heart was smashed with a sledgehammer at the sight before him. Savannah stood in the middle of her room with her parents and sister lying on the floor below her within a blood drawn circle. Candles filled the room. On the nightstand. On the dresser. In the floor. Everywhere he looked there were candles.

He trained his eyes to her parents and sister. They laid with their arms crossed and hands over top one another. Their eyes were closed. Savannah stood in the center with her back to him. She had let her hair down and it drooped in unkempt waves.

"Dear God, what have you done?"

She didn't answer. She just stood there with her shoulders slumped and staring at the floor.

He stepped closer and knelt to check the pulse of Mr. Bird. He's alive. It's like he's asleep. Jake patted his cheek but got no response. He lifted his eye lids and watched the pupils dilate. The man was comatose. Jake glanced at Mrs. Bird and Aubrey. He could see they were breathing, but it was super shallow.

He stood to his feet and studied Savannah. He side stepped to stand in front of her. Her eyes were closed but a wry grin stretched her face. It sent a shiver down his back as it was caressed with a ghostly finger. Goose flesh spread over his arms and legs. The hairs on his neck straightened.

He reached out a trembling hand toward her cheek. Her eyes flashed opened and she snapped her head towards him. She seized his hand and sank her teeth deep into his flesh. Jake screamed and yanked away from her. He felt her teeth tear through tendon and heard the bone crunch. She'd bit off his pointer finger. Taken with shock, he clutched his hand and stared at it while screaming with agony. He watched her chew on his finger as if it were a thick piece of beef jerky.

Jake held his hand close to his gut and wrapped it into his shirt to stop the spurting blood. He cursed and yelled at her, "What is the matter with you? What did she do to you?"

Savannah swallowed the finger and said with a grin, "What do you mean honey bear? It was just a love bite."

"The hell it was."

"Oh, don't be so grumpy. You should be grateful it was just one."

He stared at her and marveled at what she had become. Her eyes were black. Her voice was raspy and harsh. Her skin was pale with a purple tint. His blood oozed down her chin. He watched her lick it away as her tongue protruded out, slithering like a serpent as it had an unnatural length to it.

He crossed over to the nightstand where the victrola turntable played the record. He gave it a good kick and the music screeched to a halt.

He pulled out his necklace from beneath his shirt and clutched the cross pendant as he approached her. He watched her eyes twitch as she stared at his hand.

He crossed himself with it and uttered a quick prayer of strength. One his grandma had taught him when he was just a kid.

He looked deep into her eyes and said with conviction, "I want Savannah back. You give her back right now!"

His voice roared through the home.

She smiled at him and began to laugh. Her voice turned high as it blended into the old lady's voice. Her laughter quickly turned to that of a cackle.

A chill washed over him as he recalled the lady's laughter that night in New Orleans. He watched as her face shifted into the old lady's for a brief second like a passing shadow.

"You can't have her. She's dead. Remember?"

"No, she's not. I know she's in there. You get out of there, right now! You hear me? RIGHT NOW."

He flashed his cross at her and she hissed. Her lips peeled back to show rows and rows of teeth.

"Get out of her! Now!" He stepped closer and pressed his cross to her chest. It sizzled there as smoke rose into the air. He commanded her to leave again and pressed the cross harder to her chest. She began to shake violently. Her head snapped back, and the old woman let out a piercing shriek. A rush of air filled the room to lift the curtains and extinguish the candles. The wind whispered in the room before exiting the door it came through.

Her voice fell silent, and her body went limp.

He caught her in his arms.

His injured hand throbbed as he held her.

She rested there as if asleep.

He lowered the two of them to the floor. He brushed her hair with his good hand and spoke soothing words to her. He watched as she slowly opened her eyes. Savannah stared up at him. Her voice stuck to her throat as she asked, "What happened?"

Savannah was back.

Jake smiled and said, "It's a long story," then dialed 911.

As the already bizarre, headline gripping story was making waves across the world, the turn of recent events only added to the buzz. Upon investigation, detectives discovered that Mr. and Mrs. Bird along with Savannah's younger sister, Aubrey, were given high doses of the sleeping aid, Ambien. The ER doctors had to pump their stomachs to prevent any long turn effects. After evaluating the case and Savannah's behavior, the lead investigator suggested Savannah be placed in a mental health behavioral clinic where she could receive the proper treatment. The DA agreed. Three days later Savannah was driven up to Baton Rouge Behavioral Hospital. She was placed under a ninety-day watch and treatment plan to insure her recovery. During this time Savannah would undergo numerous evaluations to track her progress. Jake and her family were allowed to visit twice a month.

After witnessing what he had, Jake took a deep dive into various subjects surrounding Savannah's story. He researched everything from Near Death Experiences, The Lazarus Syndrome and the story in the Bible, ghosts, witches, curses, and everything in between. Late one night after having spent the evening researching and reading story after story, he stumbled upon a webpage dedicated to ghost stories of New Orleans. He found the page intriguing and spent the next half hour or more scanning its contents. He found himself nodding away in the chair. He was ready to click off his desk lamp and crawl into bed, but he made a quick swipe down the page and felt his heart skip a beat. Staring back at him from a black and white, crinkled photograph was the old lady they encountered on the street.

Her dark eyes hooked his soul, and he felt his body turn ridged. The air in the room dropped twenty degrees. His breath became labored.

Sweat beaded on his forehead. He swallowed and began reading.

Her name was Deborah Fontane. She was executed in 1947 after being tried and convicted of murder and cannibalism. She was a known gypsy and psychic who made her living reading palms and foretelling futures on the streets of New Orleans up until her arrest in 47'. Many people claimed she became entangled with witchcraft or voodoo during her later years. She went from being a kind, harmless old lady to a cold, ruthless witch. Her business quickly dwindled due to lack of clientele. From 44' to 46', countless women had disappeared only to be discovered days later partially eaten. Many claimed there must be a wild animal roaming the streets at night. Others said the devil himself was to blame. It wasn't until Deborah was caught in the act of feasting on a victim that she was arrested. She was executed less than five months after her arrest. In total, she was accused and convicted of over a dozen murders. Her death didn't stop her from roaming the streets late into the night. Countless stories had been told through the years of people spotting her wandering the sidewalks where she once conducted business.

During the spring of 54' when a serial killer had taken to the streets, many blamed the deaths on the ghost of Deborah Fontane. For years, business on that side of town suffered as her story spread. The great flooding of 62' only added to the folklore. Many were led to believe Deborah had cursed the city and all who occupied it. Rumors of her wickedness were spread again after the devastation of Hurricane Katrina as many claimed to have seen her walking up and down the streets only days prior.

Jake finished reading the page and leaned back in his chair. He glanced over his shoulder as the room seemed to hold someone other than himself. He could feel a million invisible eyes piercing the back of his head. He could almost feel a warm breath upon his neck. He shivered and gripped himself in a hug, rubbing his elbows. He saved the page to his favorites and turned his computer down for the night.

He crawled into bed and started to turn off the lamp but thought better of it.

The next day he drove over to the behavioral clinic to visit Savannah. This was only his second visit as she was still in her first month of treatment. A nurse escorted him to her room. They had to pass through a long hallway with rooms on each side. Savannah's room was at the furthest end. Screams filled the air. Some people beat upon their door and glared into the lookout glass like raged zombies. During his last visit a man had to be sedated by a husky nurse to keep him from scratching his wrists. The nurse and two others had rushed past Jake and his escort to bolt inside a room where Jake caught glimpse of blood spatter and heard the man wailing.

"You have thirty minutes. Your time begins now. Press the button next to the door when you hear the beeping."

The lady's words tug at his drifting mind. He clears his throat and nods his thanks.

The door opens with a hiss.

Savannah stands in the center of the room with her arms crossed. She smiles wide and rushes to meet him. She wraps her arms around him and squeezes his neck. Jake hugs her back.

"I'm so glad to see you. Thank you for coming."

"It's good to see you too. How are you feeling?" He asks her after giving her a kiss.

"I'm feeling better. My head is clearing from the fog. I'm able to think straight now."

"That's good."

Savannah moves a folded blanket from her bed and makes room for them to sit.

She scootches next to him and leans into his side. He places his arm around her. They talk that way for the next half hour. He debated rather he should tell her of his findings on Deborah Fontane, but ultimately decided against it. At least for now.

The beeping began. Savannah squeezed him tight and buried her head into his ribs.

They told of their love for one another and made plans for things to do once she was released.

"You know you can always take a few summer classes to make up for the lost t—"

Jake's words were cut short by sharp pain in his arm. He yelped and jumped away from her. She'd bitten his arm. His mind was instantly flooded with a flashback to when she'd taken his finger. His missing digit would forever be a reminder of that night. He pulled away and glared at her. Panting for breath and lost for words.

Savannah smiled and said with pure innocence, "What? It was just a love bite?"

The Hunted

The sun had begun to set as Matthew Johnson and his nine-year-old son, Easton, sat in their tree stand. They had been there since two-thirty and as the clock rolled closer to five, Matthew leaned in and whispered to Easton.

"We'll give it another ten minutes or so then we need to get going, okay?"

His son nodded. His black and green war paint was smeared as he'd wiped sweat and swatted mosquitoes all evening.

Matthew adjusted in his seat to relieve his aching buttocks. He watched as a squirrel in a nearby tree barked and flicked his tail at them. A crow lit on a branch and cawed. Another crow landed in the top of the tree. It craned its head and eyed them carefully.

A foul odor wafted through the air. Matthew crinkled his nose and looked down at Easton. His son snarled and looked up at him. They both were asking the same question with their eyes, *Did you do that?*

Matthew made a shew wee face and shook his head. Easton let out a faint chuckle but was quick to hide it behind his hand.

A twig snapped behind them.

Easton's eyes grew wide.

Matthew gripped the rifle and began to steady his breathing. Another stick cracked. Matthew straightened his back and gestured for Easton to remain calm.

Pop!

To their left this time. He could hear leaves crunching beneath heavy feet. *How did it get over there so quick? Must be two of them?* He thought. As he listened closer to the sound of it walking, something stood out and struck him as strange. He had a hard time making out the chi chi sound a deer makes as it trudges through the forest. It sounded more like it was on two legs rather than four. He squinted his eyes and listened again.

Two heavy thumps hit the earth as leaves crunched and branches broke. He cursed under his breath and began running a list of names of who he'd guess might be passing through the woods. If he had to bet, he figured it'd be Ben Michaels, the neighbor down the road from him. The sorry rascal always seemed to know exactly where Matthew's hunting spot was, and it never failed at least once a season for him to walk up on him and Easton in mid hunt. They had argued two seasons ago, but that didn't stop him from doing it again last year. Matthew had made up his mind, if it happens again, the man would be in desperate need of a nose straightener.

Matthew looked down to his left and peered into the thick growth. Whatever it was had stopped. The forest went eerily still. The birds quieted. The squirrels hid. Only the wind dared make a sound as it whispered among the pines.

Matthew had a cold chill come over him as he felt the hairs on his neck stiffen. The sun sank behind the trees and an enveloping shadow passed across the land. A coolness entered the air. Matthew stared at the woods, trying to see whoever was making the sounds. He grinded his teeth before finally calling out, "Ben, is that you?"

Easton huffed and snapped his head at him, "I thought we were supposed to be quiet?"

"We are, but I don't think that was a deer."

"What? What do you mean?" A dawning realization covered Easton's face and Matthew watched his brow furrow. He turned back to where the noise came from and said, "Ben, that better not be you. My daddy will whoop your tail."

Matthew elbowed Easton in the ribs and said, "Hush boy."

"Well, I'm just repeating what you said you'd do."

Matthew started to say something but thought better of it and tightened his lips. They waited for a few minutes, but never heard any more movement. The forest was still captivated in an eerie hush. It was so quiet he could hear the hum of a mosquito as it landed on the tip of his nose and dug a jack hammer into his flesh. He swatted it away, but the tip of his nose took on an instant itch.

"C'mon boy, we need to get going. It's getting dark."

"What about whoever that is walking around down there?"

"I'm sure it's nothing to worry about. Maybe it was a deer and it had a limp or something. C'mon let's get going. Your mama's going to be getting worried here soon. She's probably already got supper waiting on us."

"That was weird though don't you think?"

Matthew nodded as he slipped the rifle strap over his shoulder and moved to the ladder.

"I'll go down first. Wait until I'm at the bottom before you start coming down, alright?"

"Why?"

"Just do as I say, okay?"

"Okay."

Matthew took hold of the ladder and began the descent. He glanced up and saw Easton's paint covered face looking at him. He reached the bottom and unslung his rifle to hold it near his waist. He scanned the darkened forest and listened for any movement. Easton was making his way down when a small pebble whizzed by Matthew's head and tumbled across the ground in front of him. Matthew cursed and spun around, gripping his rifle tight.

"Alright, who's out there? What's your problem."

The woods were silent and dark.

"Easton, hurry up. Get down here."

"What was that?"

He reached the bottom and crowded close to Matthew's side. He could feel his heart pumping hard as it sped blood through his veins. The rifle was slick in his hands. He wiped a palm on the side of his pants. He searched the woods again. Nothing.

He took hold of Easton's hand and said, "We got to get out of here."

They began a brisk walk towards the trail they'd come in on. The long trail was an old logging road which became overgrown when the company went out of business some thirty years ago. Trees stretched over it to make a tunnel of branches. It wasn't for another fifty yards until the road began to snake and wind its way to a dried creek bed where Matthew's truck was parked. It would be another hundred yards from there to the main road. The distance between was nothing but a skinny trail which zigged and zagged the whole way.

They hadn't taken but a few steps along the old logging road when Matthew was hit in the back with a rock. This one almost knocked the breath out of him. He stumbled forward and found the rock rolling into the ditch. It was the size of a baseball. He grinded his teeth and snickered with anger. He looked down the trail and studied the darkness. The outcropping of a man came into view. Matthew pulled a flashlight from his back pocket and clicked it on as he said, "I don't know what the heck your problem is man, but you are—"

His words were cut short when his light beamed upon the hulking creature standing less than thirty yards from him and his son. Easton let out a blood curdling scream.

The creature turned the instant the light hit it and jutted for the tree line. Matthew could see long strands of hair float in the breeze as it strode away with an awkward gait. He felt an iron clad hand squeeze his heart and all his blood turned to ice. He could hear trees crash to the ground as the creature tore through the woods like a tank.

Easton gripped his arm until it hurt. Matthew blinked his eyes and shook his head. He slung the rifle over his shoulder and took Easton into his arms before bolting up the trail towards his truck. He dropped his flashlight and something else but didn't stop to pick it up. Easton adjusted and wrapped his arms around Matthew's neck with his legs interlocked around his waist. Easton was crying and panting for breath.

Matthew ran with all he had and thought his lungs would burst any minute now.

As he raced up the trail, he began to hear heavy footsteps pounding the earth behind him. The creature let out a deep roar as it tore after them. He could hear it grunting and breathing from a phlegm-filled throat.

"Oh Jesus."

Easton shrieked and clung tighter to his neck. He had to pat him on the back to have him loosen his grip or he'd choke.

Matthew gasped for air. His legs were like bags of wet concrete. His muscles burned and screamed with every step. He stepped on an unseen rock, and it jabbed the arch of his foot. He grimaced but kept moving forward. He had to make it to the truck. He was almost there. He has to keep moving.

The creature let out a bone chilling wail that echoed among the forest. It was so loud Matthew felt his insides rumble. Matthew and Easton pressed onward.

The creek bed was just ahead. If he looked hard enough, he could almost make out the silhouette of his truck on the other side.

The creature growled and grunted just behind his heels. Easton screamed and dug his fingers into Matthew's back.

Matthew reached into his pocket and felt for the keys.

He reached the creek bed and padded through it to reach his truck. He sat Easton on the ground and fumbled his key into the door. The lock popped and he slung the door open. Matthew could hear the creature still breathing and chasing after them. He grabbed Easton and shoved him into the truck. He shouldered his rifle and spun on his heels, pressing his back against the door of the truck.

Matthew swept the rifle side to side.

His breath came in short gasps. His eyes twitched and darted this way and that. The creature was nowhere to be found. The air was still and void of any sound. He reached behind himself and took hold of the door handle. Once inside, he turned over the ignition and shifted the truck into gear. The old Chevy pickup lurched forward, and Matthew angled for the narrow path leading to the main road.

After navigating the trail for a few minutes and catching his breath, he glanced over at Easton. The boy sat at the edge of the seat hugging himself. Matthew placed a hand on his arm and said, "Hey. You okay?"

Easton didn't answer. He only sat there gazing out the windshield. His whole body trembled.

Matthew turned his eyes to the trail only to find a black, hairy mass blocking the roadway. Matthew yanked the wheel to avoid hitting the creature. The truck skidded off the path and smacked sideways into a pine tree. The truck jarred and tossed Matthew and Easton around like rags in a washing machine. He smacked his head against the window and had stars flash before him. The back right tire blew in the process.

Dazed and shaken, Matthew could feel something warm snaking down the bridge of his nose. A searing flash of pain spread across his forehead. He touched it with the back of his fingers and winced. He could feel a gaping wound as the flesh had split from the impact he had with the window.

He reached across the seat and felt for Easton. When he couldn't feel him, he removed his fingers from his head and turned to look. Easton was lying on his back on the floorboard, moaning.

"You alright, Son? Hey. Talk to me."

"It hurts. Oh, it hurts Daddy."

Matthew noticed the passenger window was shattered and saw glass scattered in the seat and floor.

"What does? What hurts?"

"My leg. Oh. It burns."

He looked and could see a chunk of glass protruding from his pants leg. Blood was pooled around it.

He bent over to help Easton off the floor when his ears were flooded with the guttural wail of the creature. The sound blasted forth with unbelievable power and tone. The cab of the truck vibrated as the wail pierced the air. He thought it would never run out of breath. The screech went on and on and on. When it did stop, the truck jolted as the creature took hold of the hood. Its sharp nails dug and scratched into the metal. The noise raked through the air, sending every fiber of Matthew to tense with irritation. It rocked the truck once more and wailed long into the night. Easton covered his ears and whimpered. Matthew watched as the bulky creature swung back a lanky arm before crashing its hand into the front windshield. Matthew pulled Easton close and covered him with his body. Glass shards exploded every which way. The creature roared and beat upon the hood of the truck.

Easton screamed and buried himself deeper within Matthew's arms. Matthew watched the creature as it continued beating its fists upon the truck. The creature paused for a moment to gather its breath. It huffed then snapped its head around and glared at Matthew. Its eyes were like two billiards eight balls. It peeled back its rubbery lips to show rows upon rows of teeth. Its entire body was covered in thick, matted hair except for its face. The face was bare and looked like worn-out leather. Deep set wrinkles and scars snaked their way from its forehead down to its chin. Matthew was frozen as he'd locked eyes with the creature. It stared deep within his soul, searching and prodding. Its humongous nostrils flared, and its brows angled at him. A horrible stench entered the air. It was a mixture of raw sewage and soured milk. Matthew's gag reflex kicked in and he thought he would vomit right there in the truck.

The creature stood straight and beat its chest before letting out another roar. Matthew watched as it turned its back and marched into the dark woods.

Matthew let out a breath for what seemed like the first time in twenty years. Phone. He has to call Jessica. Then he'll call 911.

He patted his pocket for the phone but came up empty.

It must've jarred loose and flung out during the wreck. It's probably under the seat or something.

He searched the entire cab and felt his pulse quicken again when he didn't find it. Then it hit him. He didn't just lose the flashlight back there. There was something else he'd dropped along the road.

Please God, no. Don't tell me I dropped my phone back there.

He had to because it's not here.

"Dang it!" Matthew growled and smacked the steering wheel.

They could never make it to the main road with his truck in the shape it's in. They'd have to walk it.

His head throbbed and he touched the wound. He grimaced and wiped the fresh blood with his shirt. He turned to Easton.

"Hey. Hey, listen up. I have to carry you out of here. We won't make it in the truck. C'mon."

"No. No. Huh uh. No way. I'm not going out there. Noooo."

"Easton. We have to. C'mon." Matthew said as he tugged on his arm.

Judging by how far they'd made it along the trail, the road had to be only about seventy yards or so from where they are now. He could make a hard dash for it and flag someone down once he got there. It was either that or wait in the truck until dawn. He couldn't bear the thought of having to witness another rage fit by the creature. He couldn't put Easton through that again.

He climbed out of the truck, shouldered his rifle, and reached back for Easton.

"C'mon buddy. I got you. The road is just up there. It's not far."

Easton eyed him with suspicion and finally gave in.

With Easton wrapped around his neck again, Matthew shut the truck door, drew a breath and said, "Hang on tight, okay? We'll be there before you know it."

"I'm scared, Daddy."

"Hey. I know you are. But I'm here. I won't let nothing happen to us. I have my rifle right here. We'll be fine, alright. Now, hang on."

With that, Matthew made a dash for it.

He pounded along the jagged and crisscrossed trail. Trees and brush whipped passed them. He could hear cars driving by in the distance. Not much further.

Something stirred in the woods next to them. Trees began crashing to the ground as the monster made a break for them. He could hear it grunting and growling again as it hunted them down. Matthew pushed forward. His legs ached and his lungs were like fire, but he kept moving. He could hear the creature gaining ground. He saw the headlights of a car shine through the trees as it passed.

Easton squeezed his neck and screamed, "Shoot it! DAD! SHOOT IT!"

Matthew took hold of the rifle and set it to his hip. He spun around and back peddled. The outcropping of the creature loomed over them. Matthew squeezed the trigger. Fire blasted from the barrel and lit up the night for a mere second, but that second was enough to show the creature in all its glory. The gun blast rung his ears but he could still hear the thing when it let out another ear-piercing shriek before bolting out of sight. Matthew chambered a round and aimed in its direction. He could hear it crashing through the undergrowth and tearing away anything standing in its way. Matthew turned back for the road and raced onward. He could hear a car coming around the bend. Its lights angled with the curve and lined the woods.

Matthew began to holler.

The car passed.

"Dang it!"

He emitted out of the woods and strode to the black top. He stood at the side of the road to catch his breath. He heard the creature scream into the night. Matthew looked up into the dark sky and saw heat lightning flash in the distance. At the same moment something dug into his gut as a cramp spread under his rib cage. He winced and clutched his side, still trying to find his breath. Not seeing or hearing any cars, he began stepping down the road. The whole while he kept his eyes on the wood line. A car eventually did come along. An older man picked them up and took them to the police department, who in return, took them to the DNR's office to file a report of a bear encounter. Matthew didn't argue so as not to risk being thrown in the looney bin. He knew beyond a shadow of a doubt it was no bear but figured it would cause less of a scene if he agreed it was.

MATTHEW QUIT DEER HUNTING after that. He quit going in the woods at all for that matter. Easton didn't return to the woods until he was well in his late twenties or so. His father never liked to talk much about that night, and always agreed with the DNR report of it being a bear they encountered that night. Easton knew in his gut his father didn't really believe it, but he was too stubborn to admit anything else. It wasn't until Easton was hunting with his son some thirty years later that he knew without a shadow of a doubt what it was that had ran him and his father from the woods that night.

As Easton climbed the ladder to a hunting blind out in a field behind their house, he stopped near the top and shouldered his rifle to scan the wood line. His son, Matt, stood on the ground below him.

Easton looked through the scope and eyed the tree line. As he swiped to his right, something caught his eye. It was a dark spot among the trees that seemed out of place. It was blurry at first and Easton had to adjust his scope to bring it into focus. When the lens was righted, his heart sank into the pit of his gut. Staring back at him was a huge, bipedal ape-like creature covered from head to toe in stringy, mangy hair. Its head was rounded at the crown, and it had no neck. Its shoulders were massive and sculpted like an NFL linebacker. Easton watched it for what must've been ten seconds or more before it turned and disappeared deeper into the woods.

Easton put the rifle down and looked at his son below him.

"Hurry, get up here."

He never told anyone of what he saw.

He'd do anything if his dad were still here. He'd been the only one he would've told.

After seeing the creature watching them in the field, Easton quit deer hunting. The memories of that night with his father became all too real. From then on, he was mindful and extra careful with the kids playing outside. He forbade them from venturing into the woods and made it mandatory for them to never be alone outside after dark.

That day in the field made him wonder how many times he'd been watched like that without him ever knowing. How many times have those creatures had him within their sights?

The questions sent shivers down his spine.

He never did step back into the woods, and he never spoke of the reason why either. Like so many men before him, he carried the secret to his grave.

The eBay Killer

Jeffrey Alan Edwards, known to his boss and co-workers simply as Jeff, spends his free time operating two eBay stores named *Jeffrey's Collections* and *Jake's Treasures*. He spends most every weekend combing through yard sale tables, Goodwill shelves, and flea market booths. On occasion he takes items from victims' homes and lists them for sale on his eBay stores. Those are the sales that really get his juices flowing.

Having just sold a pair of women's Nike sneakers size six and a half, Jeff slips a pair of latex gloves on to prepare the packaging. He also wears a hair net and surgeon's mask to prevent any chance of DNA samples being discovered. Jeff began his hobby over a decade ago and so far, detectives have yet to connect anything to his eBay stores. Jeff plans for things to stay that way.

The sneakers he just sold belonged to his last victim. She was a forty-four-year-old middle school teacher from Connecticut. Of course, he had done his due diligence well in advance before choosing her as a victim. He googled her address as soon as her order came through to get an idea of the layout of her property. Liking what he saw, he then went to Facebook and found her page.

She lived alone in a small town and made for an easy target. He monitored her Facebook posts for a month before making the trip up to Connecticut. He had snuck in through the back door and entered her bedroom without her ever knowing. She was quite the screamer that one. Having finished his deed, he searched her closet for something to sell. When his eyes fell across the pair of pink Nike sneakers, he knew he'd found what he'd come for. They would make a quick sell and would lead him to his next victim.

Jeff finishes packing the shoes. The return address is to a PO Box in Florida. He would take the package to a post office in South Carolina tomorrow morning. He would be disguised as an elderly woman. He had purchased the mask from a Halloween store a few years back. He'd paid with cash as always. At the time he also bought a bald-headed man mask with a mustache. This is the one he often wears upon entering a victim's home. Although sometimes he likes to mix it up and wear another mask which he's owned for well over a decade now. The mask has big bushy eyebrows, a thick white beard and long white hair. It reminds him of Gandalf from Lord of the Rings or what he imagines Moses or God to look like. He often wears a black cowboy hat and a long trench coat when he chooses this particular mask.

He places the package on his computer desk, powers down the laptop, and crosses for his twin sized bed. No need for wasted space or resources. A twin bed suits him just fine. It also gives him more room to store his inventory. He has boxes and totes stacked four high around the bedroom. He removes his clothes and climbs beneath the silk, black sheets, fully nude. He turns on his sound machine. Tonight, he chooses the ocean. Even with the lamp lit, the room is already dark with the black painted walls and ceiling. When he reaches to turn the lamp off, the darkness consumes him. He rolls onto his back and interlocks his fingers by his naval. He awoke eight hours later in this exact position. He needs no alarm because his internal clock works just fine.

He rises and crosses to the closet. He retrieves the old woman mask and clothes. He takes a deep breath then enters the skin and character of the old lady. Afterwards, he packs a suitcase. He goes to a floor mounted safe and retrieves an envelope full of five thousand in cash, and a soft case which houses his .380. He has no intention of using it, but always brings it along in case the victim is rowdier than expected.

A few hours later after delivering the package to the post office, he's heading towards Charlotte where the package would be arriving within the next forty-eight hours. He would spend two weeks in a hotel located fifteen minutes from the victim's home. He would use the two weeks to monitor her, and her family's every move. After he received the intel he needed, he would strike.

Fast, ruthless, and precise.

Two weeks later

Near Hartford, CT

DON JAMES, LEAD DETECTIVE of the Broad Brook Police Department, sipped his coffee while strolling through a list of potential murder suspects. Bethany Henderson was murdered mercilessly in her home two weeks ago. This case has been unlike anything Don James has ever seen in all of his thirty years of working homicide. That is saying a lot considering the gory and downright evil cases he has been cursed to investigate over the years. The victim had been bound to the bed posts with each limb stretched tight by thick rope. The killer had cut off her lips and eye lids, so it looked as if she were a wild-eyed clown. He had also gutted her and left her entrails in a bag within her stomach like a coroner would do after an autopsy. The cause of death was cardiac arrest which told the medical examiner that she was most likely alive while she was cut on, meaning she either died from blood loss or terror. Either way, it sent chills down Don James's spine.

There was no sign of forced entry and nothing of value had been stolen. The victim was obviously targeted, but for what reason, Don had yet to discover. The knuckle wrap on his office door pulls him away from the computer screen. He spins around in his chair and lowers his eyeglasses to the bridge of his nose.

"You got a minute?"

Don nods and says, "Sure. What cha got?"

Steve Shilling, Don's partner, places a folder onto the desk.

"The CTV footage came back from forensics. They were able to pull about a minute clip off the DVR system. The rest was trashed," Steve said as he opens the folder. "Here are some still shots. Wendy will be emailing the complete footage over to us shortly, but here is what we have so far."

Don pushed his glasses back on and leaned close. A ghostly hand caresses his spine as he feels a chill travel down it. The image was from the camera in the living room shining past the kitchen towards the foyer. The killer was caught walking through the foyer after having stepped through the front door.

"Geez. No wonder the coroner said she may have died from being scared to death. With the creep being dressed like that, I'd of shit myself.

He looks like Moses if he'd have been around to join Jesse James's gang. There's no telling what he hid in that trench coat."

"Then there's this one." Steve places another eight by eleven image next to the first. "Look at the time stamp."

"Three o four. That's thirty minutes after he entered. That's quick considering what he did. The sorry bastard is just standing there, rubbing it in our faces." Don said as he stared at the picture of the masked killer standing in the backyard looking up at the camera while offering a friendly wave.

"Take some deputies with you and go back out there today. I want you to canvas the neighborhood and show everyone this picture. See if anyone recognizes the mask or trench coat."

"Sir, we've already spoke to all the neighbors."

"Then do it again."

Steve returned the images to his folder and said, "Whoever this is has done this before. This isn't his first rodeo. I hate dealing with the feds as much as anybody, but Don, I think it might be time to consider—"

"I already made the call. I'm waiting for the bureau to call me back as we speak." Don said as he leaned forward, propped an elbow on a knee and rubbed his tear ducts. He could feel a migraine working its way home.

Steve's surprise betrayed his face and he said, "Oh, well that's good. Maybe they can get things rolling."

As Steve was finishing his words, Don's phone began to ring.

Don sighed then motioned for Steve to leave the room. He told him to shut the door on the way out. Don picked up with a less than jubilant tone, "Detective James. Broad Brook Police Department."

"Detective James, I'm Special Agent Clark Gibson."

Don raised his head and straightened his spine.

"I received your message. I believe I may have a connection."

ANNE DECARR WASHED dishes while her husband, Daniel, was busy finding the girls a movie to watch in the living room. Anne had made homemade lasagna from her late grandmother's recipe. She heard the girls calling out different movie names as Daniel flipped through Netflix.

"I want to watch something *scary* this time," Claire had said.

"No. I'm not watching nothing scary. I want to watch a funny movie. Ooh. Stop. Go back. Yeah, the Smurf's. Let's watch that one."

"Emily, you're such a baby. You always want to watch kiddie movies."

"Hush. I am not."

Anne heard Claire make a loud fart sound with her tongue and could picture her making a face at her sister.

"Alright. Knock it off. How about the Smurf's for now, then later we can find a movie we'll all want to watch that's a little spooky. Huh, sound like a deal?" Daniel said.

"Sure. Whatever," Claire said.

"Yay. The Smurf's. Their so cute."

Daniel came back to the kitchen to help with the dishes. He rinsed while Anne dried.

"That was smooth," Anne said with a grin.

"Yeah? Kind of like when I asked you out for the first time, huh?"

"Pssh. Please, not even close. You were still a rookie back then. You're lucky I overlooked your corniness."

"Oh c'mon, cut me some slack babe," Daniel said in her ear before he kissed her cheek.

Anne smiled and continued drying.

SQUATTED IN THE BUSHES, Jefferey Alan Edwards watched Anne DeCarr through the kitchen window. She was prettier than her Facebook pictures. Which he found as odd. Usually, it's the other way around.

A mosquito buzzed in his ear. He swatted it away. A bead of sweat trickled down his forehead and landed in his mouth. He licked his lips and tasted its saltiness. He felt his heart quicken as adrenaline surged through him in anticipation of what was to come. He could feel the dopamine popping off like firecrackers in his brain. His hands and feet felt light as blood concentrated around his heart and brain. He swallowed and drew a deep breath to steady himself. He felt in his pocket and grasped the box cutter. He extended its blade then retracted it. A crooked grin twisted his face.

He adjusted his mask to better see through the slits. Anne and her Husband, Daniel, were embracing by the sink. She had her arms over his shoulders as she stared up into his eyes. He bent down and kissed her.

Jeff moved into position.

He checked his watch. It's a quarter of seven o'clock.

He waited patiently for five hours until standing and emerging from the tree line. He crept to the back door and retrieved his lock pick. Moments later it gave away and he was inside the DeCarr's home.

DON JAMES AND STEVE SHILLING were hidden in the shadows of the street, parked beneath a large oak tree. Don sipped on his third cup of coffee and was fighting the urge to pee. Special Agent Gibson and an Horry County Detective were parked three blocks behind them. Their eyes were focused on the home in the cul-de-sac.

The crackle of the radio broke the silence and gave Don a start. He almost spilt his coffee. The static clawed at his ears, and he squinted before picking up the receiver. The dispatcher said there was a body found on a street corner believed to be a byproduct of drug crime. Don cursed. As he was speaking back to the dispatcher, something caught his eye up ahead. Steve must've saw it too because he leaned closer to the windshield. Don dropped the receiver and reached for the door handle.

A man in a hood came running from around the back of the house and crossed the front yard.

Don and Steve exited their vehicles and rushed towards the home. The FBI agent and detective behind them did the same.

A gust of wind whispered through the trees. Don drew his gun and fell behind the other three. Despite being in great shape for his age, his seventy-two-year-old heart betrayed him. Not to mention the bum knee he adopted after a scuffle with a wanted fugitive a decade before. He panted for breath and trained his eyes on the subject bounding across the front yard of the home. He kept his head on a swivel, looking for any accomplice and watching the men's backs.

Detective Shilling and Agent Gibson yelled out together, "Freeze!"

The man obeyed. He nearly jumped out of his skin when the four of them surrounded him.

"Lower the hood then keep your hands where we can see them," Detective Shilling yelled.

Don watched as a teenager with a pepperoni face stared back at them. He was scared shitless.

Don cursed and lowered his weapon. The other men did the same.

"What did I do? What did I do?" the boy asked with his voice cracking.

"What's your name, son?" Don asked.

"Uh. Uh. Jacob."

"Jacob what?"

"Hunter. Jacob Hunter."

"Do you live here?"

Jacob nodded.

"How long have you lived here? You can put your hands down, just keep them out of your pockets."

"We just moved in two weeks ago."

"Where are you going this late at night?" Don asked.

Jacob licked his lips and swallowed.

Don lowered his gaze and shined his light in Jacob's face.

"A friend was coming to pick me up."

"Sneaking out of the house, huh?"

Jacob looked at the ground before asking, "What is this about? Am I in some sort of trouble or something?"

"No son, but whoever used to live here is."

Don drew a breath and turned to watch the wind rattle the lives in an old oak tree. A dog barked from the home next door. Don saw a porch light flick on followed by three others further up the street.

Agent Gibson cleared his throat and asked, "Did you ever see the man who lived here?"

Jacob shook his head, "No, he was a renter just like us. All I know is he left in a hurry. Landlord said he paid the remaining three months left on the lease in cash and had a Uhaul parked outside that same day. The neighbors said he left in the middle of the night. I've heard he was strange. What did he do?"

No one answered.

"Did he kill somebody or something?"

Again, no one answered.

"Shit, he did didn't he?"

"Go back inside kid before you get in trouble with your parents. We'll talk to everyone in the morning."

"Holy cow, this is like one of those ID shows or something. Or uh, shit, what's that other show that's always doing murder cases and stuff?"

"Forensic Files?" Steve asked.

Jacob snapped a finger at Steve and smiled, "Yeah, that one. Shit this is crazy. Dude, what if there's a body buried in the back yard? Or a skeleton hidden behind the wall?"

Don waved a hand in the air and said, "Alright. That's enough, kid. Go on now."

Jacob laughed with wild eyes and said, "This shit is crazy. I can't believe this."

As he headed back to his home, Agent Gibson looked at Don and said, "I think we're on the right track. These neighbors might know something."

Don nodded and ran his tongue along the back of his teeth. He spit to the side and said, "I want to speak with the landlord too." Don looked at the Horry County Detective and said, "And it might not be a bad idea to get the cadaver dogs here."

The detective craned his head, "Why's that?"

"In case there's a body in the back yard like the kid said."

THE NEXT MORNING WAS a Friday and the girls had slept through the shaking of their mother. Their alarm clock never did the trick. It was always Anne who was left with the task of jostling them awake. It was a little past eight thirty when Emily awoke after a bad dream. She said she dreamed she was in an old cornfield all alone and heard something rustle beside her. She screamed and began to run. The unseen being chased after her while laughing with a voice that resembled a clown. Her dream then flashed to the inside of a church where she was walking down the aisle towards a coffin. The church was empty and still. The coffin was a long way away, but she could see there was an arm draped over the side of it. As she stared and tried to make sense of who may be in the coffin, the table it was sitting on collapsed. The coffin landed at an angle and a body came rolling out to flop onto the floor. She never saw who it was. She awoke screaming.

It had caused Claire to jolt awake.

She climbed out of bed and rushed to console her sister. After getting her settled down, Emily hugged and squeezed her back before telling of the dream.

Claire felt goosebumps scatter across her flesh and for a change, she was the sister being scared. She rubbed her eyes and looked at the digital clock on their nightstand.

"It's eight-thirty-two. What in the world are we doing home? I should be taking a science test right now."

"Yeah, and I have my reading quiz this morning."

Claire put a finger to her lips and said, "Sshh. Listen."

"What is it?"

"It's quiet. Too quiet. Mom or Dad should be up by now. We should hear the coffee maker or something."

Emily drew close to her big sister and clung to her arm as the two of them crossed for their bedroom door. Claire leaned her ear against it and listened. A moment passed before she opened it. They stepped out into the hallway and listened again. Claire narrowed her gaze and wrinkled her brow at her sister. Emily gulped.

The girls crept towards their parents' room at the end of the hall. The door was shut.

Claire knocked and said, "Mom? Dad?"

No answer.

She twisted the doorknob and was frozen in place at the scene before them. Emily let out an ear-piercing wail before bolting away. Claire couldn't move. She felt a wave of nausea billow from her gut as the room was filled with a sharp copper smell. She could almost taste it in the air.

Tears welled in her eyes as she said with trembling lips, "Mom? Dad?"

They didn't answer.

THE MECKLENBERG POLICE DEPARTMENT received a call just before nine o'clock from an eighty-three-year-old widow named Elizabeth Sessions. She gave her address and said she was afraid "Somfin bad has happen" at her neighbor's house. The dispatcher could hear what sounded like two young girls crying in the background.

Authorities arrived ten minutes later to find Mr. and Mrs. DeCarr slain in their bed. From the looks of it, they were bludgeoned by a blunt force object. The room was doused in blood as if someone had taken turns splashing red paint about the room. Both victims had large Xs carved into their chests from a razor like blade.

Detective Jason Peacock spent half an hour looking over the gruesome scene before retreating outside to speak with Mrs. Sessions. She sat at the back of an ambulance wrapped in a blanket. The DeCarr girls did the same at another ambulance some thirty yards away. A female detective was squatted down in front of them asking questions as she took turns rubbing their shoulders.

Detective Peacock sighed and returned his attention to Mrs. Sessions.

"Tha girls come running and screaming up ta my door, saying they needed help. It nearly scared me ta death. I spilt my coffee and everything. I open tha door and they both come rushing in, grabbing hold of me saying I needs to call the police."

Detective Peacock nodded and scribbled notes.

"So, I took the girls over to Miss Irene's and told her to keep watch of em. I knows she keeps that shotgun of hers in the corner of her bedroom in case of a emergency. I tolds her this was one of them times. On the way to her house, I calls 911 and asks for help. Then I go back to the DeCarr's place to see for myself. The dispatcher stayed on the line with me as I entered the home. I could smell the blood as soon as I stepped through the front door. See I was an ER nurse back in my day. I knew when I smelt that there was somfin bad wrong. I had a cold chill crawl over me when I smelt it. I's go on towards the hall where the bedrooms are and the smell grow stronger. That's when I find them in theys bed all bashed up like they were."

"I see. Anybody come to mind who may have had something against the DeCarr's? Do you know if they had any enemies?"

"Lawds no. The DeCarr's was fine folks. Fine folks indeed. I's can't think of anybody who'd want to do such a terrible thing." She sniffled and looked over at the ambulance where the girls were.

"Have you noticed anything unusual within the past few days or weeks? Any strange activity? Odd cars? That sort of thing?"

She removed her glasses and pinched the bridge of her nose as she gave it some thought. Her eyes flashed wide and she looked up at Detective Peacock.

"There was a van."

"A van?"

"Yes. Lawd have mercy. I told Irene about it just last week. It was a white construction van with a ladder on the roof. It had some type of writing on the sides, but I couldn't make it out. It sat right out there in the road on two separate occasions. Acted like they was doing work or somfin, except I don't know of any neighbors having any work done. I found it strange and kept an eye on it. I couldn't much see inside except for someone moving around like they was eating lunch or somfin. I told Irene it looked like they was scoping somfin out, but she said I was just being too nosey and paranoid. I felt in my gut they was just somefin off about it. I should've listened to my instinct and had one of you to check into it." Tears filled her eyes and she swept a feeble hand towards the DeCarr's home, "Lawd I could've stopped all this. Why didn't I do somfin?"

"Sshh. Now, don't go talking like that." Detective Peacock said as he stepped forward and patted her shoulder.

She sniffled and he dug into his coat pocket to retrieve a Kleenex. He stepped back and jotted down more notes.

"Those poor youngins. Those poor poor youngins. They's too young to be without they parents. What sort of person could do such a thing?"

"An evil and sick one."

Peacock followed the lead on the white construction van, but it turned out to just be a handy man who was doing some work on a house a few streets over from the DeCarr's. The street he was working on was lacking for shade trees and the DeCarr's street was where he settled for lunch breaks the two days he was on the job.

No other lead was present. There were no prints, DNA, boot tracks, nothing. It was as if the crime was committed by a ghost or by someone well versed and experienced. Either scenario made Detective Peacock's skin crawl.

LATER THAT DAY AS Detective Don James and Special Agent Clark Gibson had spent most of their time speaking with local Uhaul owners and putting out an APB, Jeff Edwards was settling into his hotel room. He'd paid with cash of course and had used a fake name to match that of the mask he wore. The sun had set, and Jeff sat at the desk with his laptop opened. Lying next to the laptop was a red and black Craftsman hammer. He had taken his time cleaning away the blood and tissue. He was also sure to scratch out Mr. DeCarr's initials which were carved into the metal. Jeff flicked on the lamp light and took a half dozen pictures before adding them to his eBay account. He wrote out a generic description but added at the end *"Could even be used as a weapon if the need arose. Could certainly crush through bone or skull if needed."*

Jeff snickered as he typed it out. He was still smiling while he sipped his coffee. He moved onto the price and was sure to list it for an offer the right man couldn't refuse. The listing went live.

Jeff chuckled as a sly grin stretched his lips. He shook his head and closed the laptop. He shimmied out of his clothes like a snake shedding its skin, turned out all the lights and crawled beneath the covers. He was still grinning when he drifted to sleep.

One Week Later

AT EIGHT O'FIVE that morning, Jeff was called into his Bossman's office. His reason for having missed so much work in recent months was his mother's poor health. He claimed she lived with him, and he was the primary care giver. Jeff had created an elaborate story of how she had come down with some autoimmune disease that had doctors baffled and was constantly fending off pneumonia, colds, and stomach bugs. The truth was his mother had been dead for years. He had taken care of that issue long ago. She was always the nagging type anyhow, and after coming home late from doing a dirty deed, her nagging had pushed him over the edge. Long story short, she's now peacefully buried in the basement under five hundred pounds of concrete.

"Jeff. Jeff. Hey, are you with me?" His boss said as he waved a hand in front of Jeff's face.

Jeff cleared his throat and scratched his forehead.

"Uh, yeah. Sorry. You were saying?"

His boss sighed and shook his head.

"What am I going to do with you?"

Jeff massaged the wooden arms of the chair and glared at the short ball headed man with a pudgy gut. He reminded him of George Constanza from Seinfeld. He watched as the man stood from his chair and crossed to a window looking out to the work floor. Machines wined and hummed as men moved about the building like ants.

Jeff's eyes began to wander about the room, searching for something heavy enough to crack through skull. The boss continued talking, but Jeff wasn't listening. He was too busy searching. He settled on a marble bookend carving of a grizzly bear. The thing had to have some weight to it. He had watched the Bossman maneuver it along the bookshelf before and noticed how it seemed to sit heavy in his chubby hand. He could pounce and be on the man before he ever knew what hit him.

The Bossman stopped talking and turned around to face him. Jeff diverted his eyes from the marble sculpture and refocused his attention.

"Well?"

"I'm sorry, what was the question?"

The Bossman glared at him and began to grind his molars.

The air grew thick between them. The room suddenly became muggy and humid.

"I'm going to say this once, and I will not be repeating myself. You have thirty days to clean up your act or you will be replaced. Is that understood, Jeff? Do I make myself clear?"

Jeff tightened his jaw and nodded.

"Good. Now get out of my office."

As Jeff stood from the chair, his phone pinged with a notification. He exited the room and retrieved his cell. He swiped down and felt a surge of adrenaline rush through him. His muscles quivered with excitement.

The hammer had sold.

He swallowed hard and felt his breath quicken. He clicked on the details and scrolled down to see where the buyer was located.

Beaumont, Texas. Henry Janson.

Jeff smiled as a sense of giddiness washed over him. He pocketed his phone, inserted his ear buds, and returned to the work floor. He could hardly wait to get home and package the item. He'd spend most of the night researching Henry

Janson and the layout of his home. If he shipped the hammer out first thing in the morning, the man should have it by Wednesday or Thursday. That would allow Jeff to leave Friday after work and if he drove it straight through, he could be in Beaumont by Saturday afternoon. He could grab a bite to eat, take a quick nap at a truck stop, do the deed that night and be back by late Sunday in time for work on Monday.

Sure, it would be a quicker process compared to what he'd much prefer, but with the Bossman cracking down on him, he could not afford to miss any more work or he would be at risk of raising suspicions. He could continue to do his side hustle, but it would require less time for research and stalking. As long as he kept every scene different without leaving clues, signatures, or MOs, no one would ever catch on to him.

Would it be riskier this way?

Of course.

The added risk added to the thrill of it all, and that was what made his side hustle so fulfilling.

HENRY JANSON IS A retired long haul truck driver of twenty-three years according to his Facebook profile. He had his seventieth birthday just last month. Jeff counted over two dozen birthday wishes on his Facebook page. Little did all those friends and relatives of his know that

that would be his last. The reaper had come bearing his scythe, and tonight Henry's soul was Jeff's to take. Jeff smiled at the thought as he hid behind a tree in the old man's backyard. It was a quarter past midnight, and Jeff had been watching since dusk. The old man lived alone. At least it seemed that way. There was no lady friend on his Facebook and by the looks of it, his wife had died some years back. There was one vehicle in the driveway. A silver Honda Civic. Jeff had watched Henry let the small, terrier looking dog out to pee two hours earlier before turning out all the lights.

Despite the man's age, he would be a challenge. Henry Janson was much larger than Jeff himself. He was a thick, barrel-chested man and had Popeye like forearms. Jeff reached a hand into his pocket and touched his .380 pistol. He had no intention of using it on the man, but should the need arise, Jeff took comfort in knowing it was there.

He draws a deep breath, shuts his eyes, raises his face to the full moon, and exhales slowly. He feels the dopamine surge through him in anticipation of what is to come. He stands and bounds on the balls of his feet like an octagon fighter. He cranes his neck side to side, and it gives off a sick crack. A wry smile stretches his lips, and Jeff emerges from the wood line.

THE JEFFERSON COUNTY Police Department received a well fare call for Henry Janson five days later. His daughter in Washington State had been unable to reach him for the past few days. Due to their close relationship, she knew something was wrong when her father had failed to respond to her calls and texts.

A sheriff deputy responded to the home around nine that morning. He knocked on the door and cupped his hands on the windows. He saw and heard no movement despite Mr. Janson's car being in the driveway. The officer did notice a foul odor and considering the circumstances it was enough for him to make his way inside. The odor grew louder as he made his way towards the back bedroom. With his gun drawn, the deputy placed his back to the wall and slid down the hall. He noticed blotches on the carpet near the doorway of the bedroom. The tan carpet looked to have been bleached in several places.

The deputy trained his pistol and entered the bedroom. He felt his heart thud when his eyes took in the outcropping of a body lying in bed. Blood spatter was everywhere. The deputy tucked his nose beneath his shirt and swallowed hard to keep the vomit at bay. The decomposed body of Mr. Janson lied atop the comforter with his arms crossed over his chest as if his killer had prepared him for burial. The deputy felt a cold hand sliver down his spine at the thought. Tilting his head against his shoulder and speaking through his shirt, the deputy called it into dispatch. Within minutes, back up arrived. Half an hour later detectives and CSI were on scene.

ONE CSI WORKER, Melissa Shelby, had been an investigator for Jefferson County for the past twelve years. Prior to her time in Jefferson County, Melissa was a part of the CSI crew in Broad Brook, CT. She had often worked alongside Don James and the two had become good friends through the years. They even dated for a short while at one point.

The two still kept in touch and had actually spoke just last week when Don had called to tell her about his struggle in tracking the ruthless killer of a lady there in Broad Brook. The two had talked about the crime scene for an hour that night. Don often called her when he had trouble piecing things together. One thing he had told her that stood out was the way the killer had *gutted* the lady as if preparing her for the coroner. The way Don described it and the way he worded it, had really stood out to her. With that in mind, when Melissa Shelby walked into Mr. Janson's bedroom and found him lying there with his arms crossed like he'd been prepared for his funeral, she couldn't help but go back to her and Don's conversation.

Could this be the same guy? There's no way. Has to just be a coincidence.

These thoughts played through her head as she combed over the scene. In the far corners of her mind, she kept repeating a phrase she had heard Don say over and over during her time at Broad Brook, *There are no such things as coincidences. Two plus two will always equal four.*

As she examined Mr. Janson's body, she noticed the ligature marks around his neck. It was obvious he had been strangled with some type of cord. She pulled away from the body and did a slow scan of the room. One thing that immediately grabbed her attention was the lack of a bedside lamp next to where Mr. Janson was laying. The nightstand on the other side had one. Melissa angled around the bed and went to examine the lamp. It wasn't an ordinary lamp. It appeared to be an antique. It had a cherry wood base and from that base rose a fly rod that bent over like a question mark. A wooden rainbow trout hung from the tip of the rod. On top of the bent rod was an extension where the bulb and shade were. A long black cord ran from the base and went behind the bed. Had the killer used the other lamp and discarded it? If he used the lamp to kill him, why stab him so many times? Had he tied the man up prior to killing him? As Melissa ran these questions through her mind, she went back to the doorway and spoke to another CSI worker who was busy taking samples from the bleached carpet. It appeared the killer must've cut himself as so many do in such violent attacks. In a frantic attempt to clean things up, he doused bleach where there must've been blood droplets. If they're lucky, there may be a trace amount of DNA left.

"He did a pretty good job with the cleanup, didn't he?"

"Yeah, but I'm hoping there's enough down deep in the fibers for us to pull from." The CSI worker told Melissa.

"Good. Put a rush on that, will you? I think I may be on to something. I need to make a call."

The CSI worker paused her work and looked up at Melissa from a squatted position. "Really? Whacha got?"

"Let me call my friend in Connecticut first. I'll fill you in when I get off the phone. Do your best to pull DNA from that sample." Melissa finished as she made her way down the hall and out the front door.

AROUND TEN O'CLOCK, Don James was seated at his desk when Melissa's call came through. He smiled when he saw the name light up on his phone.

"Tell me something good, girl. I need some good news for once."

"I think I can do that."

Don chuckled, "What are you up to?"

"I'm investigating a homicide."

Don sipped his coffee and watched the wind rustle the leaves outside.

"Go on."

"No sign of forced entry. Not a robbery. Seems to be personal or ritualistic."

Don leaned forward in his chair and sat his coffee down.

"What do you mean *ritualistic*?"

"It reminds me of what you said about your lady there in Broad Brook."

Don gulped and blinked his eyes.

"I'm listening."

"Our victim was found in bed with his arms folded over his chest as if *prepared* for burial."

That word *prepared* reverberated through his mind like a pinball.

"He has deep ligature marks around his neck which could have very likely been enough to crush his windpipe and block any airflow, but he was also stabbed twenty-seven times."

Don cursed on the other end.

"It appears our perp may have cut himself in the process. We are working to extract blood samples from the carpet, but the damn bastard used bleach where he leaked out."

The line grew quiet for a moment.

"Something else that grabbed my attention was a missing lamp by the bedside. The one that's there appears to be an antique of sorts. I remember you mentioning that your victim was big into antiques. Didn't you tell me that?"

"Did I? I don't recall that I did."

"Yeah, remember you talked about the old pictures and artifacts. You said she had good taste."

"Yeah, she did."

"I know it may seem like a stretch to connect this, but like you've always said, two plus—"

"Two will always equal four. Yeah, guilty as charged."

"There are no coincidences. If these cases are connected somehow, the victim's love for antiques may be the link."

"Where do antique lovers like to shop?" Don wondered aloud.

"Well, yard sales for one. Flea markets. Facebook marketplace. Craigslist. eBay. I'm no antique expert, but besides looking around at the antique stores I think these are places they would all have in common."

"Most of those places you just mentioned would be bound to a local area. If a murder in Connecticut is going to be connected to a murder in Texas, there must be a thread online somewhere."

"Yeah, you're right. eBay then."

"It sounds like a long shot, but I think it'd be worth looking into. We could pull their bank records to see if either of them had purchased anything from eBay recently and try to see if there is a related account they bought from." Don said.

"Sounds like a bread trail worthy of following."

"Thank you, Melissa. I'm sending Agent Gibson a message now. Keep me apprised of the situation there in Beaumont, and I'll do the same here."

"10-4."

JUST BEFORE MIDNIGHT, Jeff was busy showering and preparing for bed. He did his best to keep his cut hand away from the water. On a few occasions water snaked down his arm and stung him on the raw meat. He cursed and gritted his teeth each time. Stepping out of the shower, Jeff wrapped a towel around his waist, wiped condensation from the mirror, and sat upon the sink counter. He opened a bottle of rubbing alcohol with his teeth, took a deep breath, and poured it over the wound. His jowls quivered and beads of sweat broke out on his forehead. Jeff groaned and continued pouring. He finished, balled his hand into a fist, and cursed again through clinched teeth. Jeff retrieved a bandage and a roll of white gauze tape from his first aid kit. He wrapped his hand then headed for the bedroom where his laptop waited for him on the desk.

Still wrapped in the towel, Jeff took a seat at the desk and booted up the laptop. He connected to the motel's WIFI and logged into his eBay account. He had all the pictures of Mr. Janson's lamp already downloaded. He uploaded nine of them and wrote out a brief description of the item. He ended the description by saying, *The cord is long enough you could probably strangle your mother-in-law with it. Just kidding. It is a really long cord though.*

Jeff snickered as he clicked the button to list it. The item went live, and he couldn't help but smile. His next victim would surely be coming along soon. It was a fine lamp, and it did indeed have a really long cord. Jeff chuckled and stood from the desk. He powered down the laptop, dropped his towel, and slithered beneath the covers. He fell asleep smiling and thinking of how that cord felt in his hands as Mr. Janson struggled for his life. He may just have to use that lamp twice. At least once more then he'd move on to something else. He could hardly wait for a buyer. Something about the cord on that lamp had stirred a craving in him. He liked the way he could feel his victim struggling and fighting for life. It had sent a thrill and extra dose of dopamine through him unlike anything else. He couldn't wait to do it again on the next buyer.

DON JAMES AND AGENT GIBSON had spent the last few days working with both the bureau and Broad Brook Police Department on combing through the victim's bank records for any purchases made from eBay. It hadn't taken long to find it in the statements. Both victims had bought items from eBay shortly before their murders. The first victim had purchased an antique painting from eBay one month prior to her murder. The victim in Texas had bought a craftsman hammer from eBay only days before his murder. A few hours after making the discovery on the bank records, the IT and Cyber Security team was able to log into both victims' eBay accounts and discovered they had both made their purchases from a store called *Jeff's Collections*. Melissa was right. Two plus two does equal four. After sorting out the account's listed items, the most recent item listed was an antique lamp. Don snapped a picture of it and sent it to Melissa. She confirmed it as the mate to the one found in Mr. Janson's home.

"The sorry bastard is taking items from his victim's homes and reselling it to new victims.

And look at what he says in the damn description. Did you read that?" Don asks.

Agent Gibson stands behind the IT worker's chair with his arms crossed and a finger over his lips. "Yeah, I see that. He rubs it right in our faces."

"So instead of hunting his victims, he's luring them to himself. He's like a damn snapping turtle."

Agent Gibson wrinkles his brow, "Like a what?"

"I said he's like a snapping turtle. Growing up poor in the south, I've had my fair share of cooter stew. I remember one day when I was watching my daddy butcher and prepare one for supper, I noticed it had this worm looking thing in the bottom of its mouth. I asked my daddy what it was and he said it was what the turtle used to lure the fish into its mouth. He said that turtle would find a nice spot on the bottom of the lake, open his mouth wide, and wiggle that little piece of meat so it looked like a worm. A little ole fish would come along thinking he had himself an easy meal but before he even knew what happened, that turtle had done clamped his jaws down on it. That's what our killer has been doing to these people. Instead of going out on the hunt like most killers, he used this eBay store to lure his victims to himself."

The room went quiet.

Don could see Agent Gibson was thinking.

Their eyes met. They were thinking the same thing. Two can play this game.

JEFF DIDN'T HAVE TO WAIT long. Three days after listing the lamp, he got the notification on his phone that the lamp had sold. While on his lunch break, he checked to see who bought it and where they were located. Melody Stensland from Ohio was the buyer. He did a quick glance at her Facebook and was happy to see she was another middle aged, single lady. Certainly makes his job a little easier. He googled the address and switched to the street view. It was a decent single-family home. Probably thirteen hundred or so square feet. It wouldn't give her much room to run, which once again, would make things a little easier.

After going back to work from his break, the rest of the day his mind was focused on completing his new task. He ran scenarios through his head, plotted out a step-by-step plan, and estimated the hours and miles it would take to drive there and back. If he went home and packaged the item so he could ship it out first thing in the morning, the lady should receive it by Tuesday of next week. That would give him a few more days to do his research. He thought about doing like he did with the Janson murder and do the deed over the weekend, but he was afraid of creating a pattern. He decided it would be best to make the nine-hour drive Wednesday right after work. He would call in sick Thursday before making the drive back into town after having done the deed early that morning, likely sometime around two or three am.

Jeff could hardly wait to get home so he could pack the lamp for his new victim.

FROM THE MOMENT Don and the investigators purchased the lamp, using the account of a friend of a woman at the department, they positioned FBI agents and local police to watch the place over the following days and weeks. However long it took for the killer to arrive, they were prepared to wait it out. Don and Agent Gibson were on scene and communicated through radio. The lamp had arrived at the woman's home yesterday afternoon. The past five days since the item was purchased had preceded without any sign of their killer. However, since the lamp was delivered, everyone's senses were on high alert.

It was just after nine o'clock on Wednesday night when Don radioed into Agent Gibson.

"Anything?"

A moment passed before Gibson's gruff voice came back through the static, "Nothing yet. Keeping our eyes peeled on the south entrance. My gut says that's the way he'll approach."

"10-4."

AN HOUR LATER and Jeff had reached his position. He squatted in the shrubbery and peered past the branches to peek through the kitchen window. Most of the lights were still on and he had caught a glimpse of Melody filling a glass of water by the sink. She had long blonde hair that rested over the shoulder of her white robe. The room was dimly lit and cast a shadow over her face. He could only see her from the shoulders to her waist. He grinned and breathed deeply through his nose. The dopamine surged through his veins and caused every muscle to quiver. He felt electric. Like there should be sparks emitted from his fingertips. The rush and thrill of it all was settling over him and he knew it wouldn't be long before the deed would be performed. He checked his watch, *10:41*. He would wait until after one to enter. As long as he was back on the road by two, he'd have plenty of time to get back to South Carolina by tomorrow morning. He had to control his breathing as the excitement was overwhelming him.

Stay calm. You got this. Breathe Jeff. Breathe, he told himself.

A mosquito dug into his neck, and he slapped his flesh. It gave off a loud smack. He heard a dog bark in the distance. A cricket whirred next to him. He grinded his molars and stared in its direction, wishing it were dead. He narrowed his brows and felt hot breath steam from his nostrils. The cricket must've felt his energy because it suddenly went quiet. Jeff smiled and began to chuckle. He turned his attention back to the Stensland home and waited.

AT ONE O'SEVEN Jeff made his way in through a side door. He removed his boots like a gentleman and walked with socked feet to keep the noise down. The house was pitch black and silent. Jeff knew by her Facebook account she was single with no kids. Again, things that only made his job easier. A part of him felt guilty for doing something so easy. He sort of wished this one would have put up more of a challenge. At least he could re-use the lamp again. That would make it all worth it. Maybe his next victim will present greater difficulty and require him to up his game.

He kept his eyes peeled for potential items he could use in the future as he crept through the darkened home. He was sure to walk along the walls to avoid the floor from creaking. The master bedroom was adjacent to the living area. Jeff watched his black shadow pass across the television screen. As he neared the bedroom door, he reached back instinctively to feel for his .380. He had no plans of using it tonight, but as always, it was reassuring to know it was there if needed. He then slid his hand to the buck knife on his hip. The plan was to take her life with the lamp cord if it were next to the bed like he'd hoped. If it weren't, he'd hold her at gunpoint until she showed him where it was. The idea of using the knife to take a finger or ear had crossed his mind also. He figured it'd be something else to add to the mix to keep things different.

He reached the bedroom door and pressed his back to the wall. The door was cracked halfway and open enough for him to slither through. He slid his feet across the hardwood and stood just inside the door frame. There she was lying in bed with the covers clinched tight around her face. The room was too dark to really see her features, but he could see the outcropping of her disheveled hair. Jeff felt his heart knock hard against his ribs. He licked his lips and swallowed hard. He diverted his eyes to the nightstands and felt a surge of adrenaline when he saw it. There it is. Waiting for him. Waiting for him to wrap the cord around her neck like a snake and squeeze the life from her.

His pulse began to soar.

His breathing quickened.

He stepped forward.

There was movement. The bed stirred.

The covers flew back in such a flash his mind had no time to process what was happening. A bright ball of fire filled the room followed by three rapid explosions.

He dove to the floor at the foot of the bed. His shoulder slammed into the hardwood. A flash of hot searing pain stung him in the side of his gut.

The dumb witch shot me. I'll be damned.

He placed a hand to his side and felt warm blood slip between the webbing of his fingers. He heard her stand from the bed. Jeff squirmed backwards across the floor while reaching for his .380 with the other. Voices could be heard outside. Static from a radio crackled somewhere. He reached the wall and had just found purchase of his weapon when the person who shot him stepped around the corner of the bed and yelled, "Hands. Let me see your hands."

Jeff didn't move. He stared through the darkness. His mind tried to process what was taking place. The voice was that of a man. An older man at that.

What the hell?

He'd been set up.

"Show me your damn hands, now!"

Jeff began to chuckle. He watched as the man removed the wig and tossed it to the floor. Jeff released the grip on his .380 and raised both hands in a defenseless gesture.

"You piece of shit. Why I ought to end your worthless life right now. You're a waste of air you know that?"

"I wish you would. Just get it over with. I'll even reach behind my back so you'll have justification for your actions. What do you say? Want to see who's got the faster draw? Hell, I'm even giving you a head start."

"You move a damn inch, and I'm emptying this magazine right into your friggin face. Don't test me."

Jeff grinned big enough to show his teeth. He stared at the man long and hard. Another voice crackled over the radio. Footsteps could be heard pounding closer outside. Jeff made a break for it. Instead of going for the pistol on his right side, he went to the knife on his left. The man began firing on him. He had only gotten off two shots before Jeff managed to retrieve the blade and flick his wrist to send it sinking into the man's hip. The man yelped but kept firing. Jeff took two rounds. One to his right shoulder and one to his left elbow. He felt the bones shatter and fragment. Jeff dove to his right to hide on the other side of the bed. He reached behind him and gripped his pistol. He stood from his crouched position and took aim of the man. The man was doing the same to him. They both began to fire.

The room lit up in bright flashes.

The shots reverberated off the walls.

AGENT GIBSON POUNDED through the home, racing towards the bedroom. The SWAT team was just ahead of him. He heard the shots and seen the bedroom window light up as he rushed for the front door. The home was silent when they entered except for the booming voices and charging feet of the SWAT team and other officers.

They barged through the bedroom. Smoke hung in the air and the smell of gunpowder was so thick you could taste it. Someone flicked on the light. Blood spatter littered the walls. Gargled breathing came from the right. Agent Gibson looked down to find Detective Don James lying on his back with blood bubbling from his mouth. The SWAT team rushed past them and focused their attention on the other side of the bed where the suspect lay in his own pool of blood. After hearing them bark out commands, Agent Gibson heard one of the officers finally announce there was no pulse.

Gibson applied pressure to the wound in Don's chest and tried to soothe him as he called the others for help. Don locked eyes with Gibson and started trying to talk. Gibson leaned close.

"He's not...not..." more heavy and gargled breathing. "He's not...alone. Someone...someone...else."

Gibson pulled back and yelled out, "Secure the perimeter. Clear the house. Now!"

He felt Don clinch his arm. He looked back to the dying man. Don shook his head. Gibson squinted his eyes.

"Not here. An acq...uain...tance."

Gibson felt his heart drop at the word. How did Don know. Had the killer revealed something in his final moments?

Gibson watched the life fade from Don's eyes and felt him release the grip on his shirt. Don's labored breathing ceased, and he rested his head against the floor. His glazed eyes glared at the ceiling. Clotted blood leaked from his mouth.

Gibson cursed and rubbed a hand over his face before standing to his feet. It should have been him used as bait. He should never have listened to Don and let him take on such a risky mission at his age. Don had told Gibson he had less to lose. Gibson was the one with a wife and kids. Don was divorced with no kids. If one of the men were to die in this fight, Don had refused for it to be Gibson. He was proud to take on such a duty and absolutely refused the offer of anyone else. This was Don's job. He was the one who had brought them all into this and if anyone were to be taken out, it was going to be him.

Gibson shook his head as he recalled Don's words during the briefing only days before.

Paramedics rushed into the room and Gibson stood over them and watched as they tried to resuscitate the man. Gibson followed them out as they rushed Don away on a gurney with an oxygen bag over his bloodied face. Gibson road with him in the back of the ambulance. Don was pronounced dead before they even reached the hospital.

Gibson couldn't shake the last of Don's words.

Why did he think there was someone else?

What had the killer said to make him think that?

Three Months Later

INSIDE THE HOME where Jeffery Alan Edwards once lived, Jacob Hunter sits at a desk in the dark. His laptop is booted up and glows upon his face. It's just after two in the morning and he had one more item to list before calling it a night. He uploads the pictures, writes the description, and gives it a price. The item goes live. Jacob logs out of *Jake's Treasures* and turns off his laptop. He undresses and crawls beneath the covers fully nude. The pair of running shoes shouldn't take long to sell. He could hardly wait to get started. If he listened closely, he thought he could hear the spirit of Jeff's mother calling out from the basement, begging him not to pick up where Jeff had left off. Too late for that because things had already been put into motion. Jeff's contingency plan was laid out with perfect directions and Jacob was determined to follow them to the tee. He grinned at the thought.

An hour later, he heard his phone ping.

He rolled over and checked it.

The shoes had already sold. Some lady from Arkansas.

Yes, the plan had been put into action and the universe was rewarding him for following Jeff's orders. He'd do his research in the morning. He'd never been to Arkansas. But there's a first for everything, right? He snickered and fell back to sleep with a long grin stretched across his face.

Somethings out There

As I grow older, I find myself questioning things I used not think twice about. Such as why dogs tend to only live for a dozen or so years, yet a dang turtle can live upwards of a dozen decades. I mean what the hell is up with that? I also have begun to wonder what this world will be like when my kids are grown. It's scary to think of, and I try not to but sometimes, damn it, I just can't help it. Kind of like I how I can't stop thinking of what happened to me and my cousin once when we were young. I've never really told anyone about it before, so I figured I'd write it all down and let you the reader decide for yourself. I've always been better at expressing myself through written words anyhow. I hope one day, when my children are grown and the world isn't quite what it used to be, that maybe they can come back to this story and get lost in a world that once was.

"MAKE SURE TO BRING your glove with you. I've been practicing my two seamer. You won't believe how much it moves now."

My cousin Matt had said over the phone.

We had both started playing baseball the year before. I mostly played second base or left field when I wasn't pitching. Matt was our short-stop and star pitcher. He was a hard throwing righty that kept hitters on their toes. I remember watching this one poor kid with tears running down his cheeks as he had trouble gripping the bat with his trembling hands. He struck out on three pitches of course. He swung at everything Matt threw and if he was lucky, he may have come within a foot of putting the barrel on the ball. I think he struck out on purpose just to get the at bat over with.

Me and Matt were more like brothers than cousins. We played baseball and basketball together and spent pretty much every weekend at one or another's house. We never once argued or fought. That's the Gods honest truth.

This one weekend though, I'll never forget.

It was my turn to spend the night at his house. I remember I couldn't wait to get home from school that Friday so I could pack and have my mom drive me over to Matt's place. We talked about our plans all week at school. We shared second and third period together and always sat with each other for lunch. We made plans to camp out in his backyard and tell ghost stories by the fire. Ride the four-wheeler in the field behind his house before going fishing at Mr. Gann's pond. It was stocked with bass and catfish the old man caught from the lake. We also talked about what scary movies we wanted to watch on the night we didn't sleep in the tent. We loved thrasher movies and creepy mysteries. Our favorites were Jeepers Creepers, The Mummy, Texas Chainsaw Massacre, and the like. I bet we watched those films over a dozen times a piece, but still got a start at each jump scare. We also loved watching Dumb and Dumber and The Nutty Professor. Our favorites were always the scary movies though.

As soon as my mom pulled in our driveway, I bolted out and raced to my room to finish packing. I had packed most of my stuff a few days before hand. I just had to add some fresh underwear, socks, and be sure I had my ball glove and that my tackle box was ready to go.

I made it over to my cousin's house late that afternoon and the first thing we did was throw the baseball. I remember it was early October some time because the leaves were just beginning to change colors and the fall weather was settling in. The days were mild and sometimes warm without a fall breeze, but the mornings and nights would often get down to low fifties or high forties.

As we tossed the ball back and forth, the leaves fluttered in the trees with a handful losing their grip and drifting in the wind. Birds sang over us, and two crows cawed from the ridge of the house.

"Hey, did I tell you about Jenna laughing at my joke the other day?" Matt asked as he caught my throw near his chest.

I shook my head, "No, but please tell me you didn't tell her the one about the looneys chanting numbers over the fence."

He smiled and threw back a two seamer that popped me right in the palm. I winced and shook away the sting.

"That's such a lame joke, dude. You can do better than that." I said as I returned the favor with a two seamer of my own. It didn't move as much as his, but he caught it in a bad spot too.

"What's wrong with it? You laughed when I told it to you?"

"I mean yeah, it's funny and all, but I thought you would have done better than that."

He started laughing at a thought I could see him channeling. He looked at the ball and fiddled with a grip before throwing one back near my ankles.

"What are you laughing at?"

"I'm just picturing the poor dude getting poked in the eyeball for being too nosey. I think there might be a life lesson in there somewhere."

I chuckled and said, "Yeah, don't stick your eyeball to a hole in a fence belonging to the insane asylum. Maybe you can do a speech when we graduate high school."

We both laughed and continued throwing the ball.

A half hour later, my aunt called us in for supper.

She had made Sloppy Joes and we licked our plates clean.

After supper we retreated to Matt's room and played a few games on the PlayStation. We liked football, baseball, and army games. After a few rounds of that we settled for popcorn and a scary movie. We started with Jeepers Creepers then switched to Chainsaw Massacre. It was probably halfway through the second movie that we both began drifting to sleep. We turned in for the night sometime around one o'clock. I remember hearing my uncle come home from second shift about an hour before falling asleep.

We woke up the next morning around seven-thirty to the tune of Matt's alarm. He had downloaded a whistling bomb sound effect without telling me and it nearly gave me a heart attack. I thought we had been nuked or something. He got a good belly laugh when I nearly scrambled out of bed. I gave him a frog on his arm for compensation.

The savory aroma of bacon and eggs hung in the air, and I could hear voices in the kitchen. My uncle loved to cook and always made the best bacon and egg sandwiches.

"What cha want to do today? Still want to ride the wheeler in the field? I can hook up the old canoe to it like last time." Matt said as he changed shirts.

I nodded, "Yeah that sounds fun. Maybe we could fish after that."

"Yeah, I got a new spinner bait I picked up last week when me and Dad went to Bass Pro. I've been dying to try it out ever since. I want to try that pond in the woods out there. Dad don't want us venturing that far, but I would bet my left nut there's some monster's over there."

"Boy, you crazy." I laughed before adding, "Why don't he want us over there? That's still part of Mr. Gann's land, isn't it?"

"I don't think so. I kind of think it might still belong to whoever lived in that old house on the hill over there."

"Oh. Well, who did live there?"

"I think it was Mr. Gann's Mama and Daddy's place, but I think his sister sold it after they died. That's why Mr. Gann hates his sister so much. Somehow, he says she sold it without his permission or something. Whoever bought it just sat on it and ended up letting it rot. I heard there was a hermit living in it at one time. That's why Dad don't want us over there, I guess. But I mean, he'd never know if we ventured over there, right?"

I tightened my lips and craned my head.

"We'll think about it then, won't we?"

"Yeah. Sure." I said.

After changing clothes with our backs to each other we made our way into the kitchen. Aunt Amy was leaning against the counter while flipping through a home décor magazine and talking about paint colors. Uncle Trace was busy scrambling eggs over the stove.

Aunt Amy looked up from the magazine as we came into view. She smiled and said, "Morning night owls. Y'all sleep good?"

I smiled and nodded.

Uncle Trace turned around and said, "Hey boy."

"Hey Uncle Trace."

"Figured y'all could use one of my bacon and egg sandwiches to start your day." He said with a big grin. His short black hair was spiked in the front as always. He wore a silver chain beneath his white t-shirt with a blue and white flannel long sleeve over that. It was tucked into his khaki cargo pants.

I always had such a good time over at Trace and Amy's. Me and Matt were always finding something to do. If by chance we ever got bored, Uncle Trace would often take us to the flea market or to Chimney Rock to look for arrowheads and try our luck at trout fishing. There was always something fun to do. It was never a dull moment when we were all together.

"Matt, we need to make sure you take your Lantus before y'all start playing. Probably need to go ahead and give it to you. Breakfast is almost ready anyway," Aunt Amy said to him as she sat the magazine down and reached into the fridge for a vile of liquid. A box of needles rested next to the fridge.

I remember we were at the flea market when Matt found out he was a juvenile diabetic. Uncle Trace is a bad diabetic himself, so when Matt couldn't stop going to the bathroom every fifteen minutes or so, Uncle Trace got suspicious. We first thought it was the Sundrops he'd drunk earlier that morning and quickly blamed it on those, but after Matt's fourth trip to the men's room in less than an hour, Uncle Trace knew something was wrong. We came home early that day and Uncle Trace brought out his sugar checker. He pricked Matt's finger, and the darned reader wouldn't read his sugar. They tried it again with another checker and got the same result. Aunt Amy hopped on the phone to call the doctor. The doc said they needed to get Matt to the hospital asap. Once there, the doctors checked his sugar and found out it was in the low five hundreds and climbing. That was two years ago.

Amy finished giving him the shot. He rubbed his belly and stuck his tongue out at me when saw me watching. I laughed and turned to look out the sliding glass doors. Outside was a large back deck overlooking an in-ground pool and a fenced in yard. Beyond the fence was a thick grove of pines followed by cut fields. Four-wheeler trails snaked their way here and there, leading to the fields and fishing ponds of Mr. Gann's

I remember I still had a bad case of a poison oak rash behind my right knee. I caught myself scratching at it as I stared out the window at the woods. My mom had sent my prescription of prednisone with me, and I was to take it twice a day with a meal. I figured I'd take it with breakfast, then take it again with supper.

"How's your poison oak doing, James?" Aunt Amy had asked me as she noticed me scratching.

I'd popped a few crusty bumps and would later regret it. I looked up at her and said, "It's getting a little better. Still aggravates the snot out of me but not as bad as it did."

"That's good. Just try not to scratch it. I know it's easier said than done, but you'll only make it spread the more you scratch at it."

"I know. That's what Mama told me. I try not to, but sometimes I forget and just start going to town on it."

Matt said, "I told him if he had a dollar for every time he catches that stuff, he could retire before he finished high school."

We all shared a laugh at that. It was true though. All I had to do was look at a leaf of it and I'd catch it. Hell, sometimes all I had to do was think about it and it'd somehow start. I'm allergic to it now as an adult, but not near as bad.

"Alright folks, get it while it's hot." Uncle Trace announced as he shoveled the eggs onto a big plate. We each made our own bacon and eggs sandwiches. A rerun of Andy Griffith played over the small TV in the corner above the dining room table. We laughed and downed the delicious sandwiches.

"What you boys got planned for the day?" Aunt Amy asked as she tossed a braid of her blonde hair over a shoulder.

Me and Matt looked at each other.

Matt turned to her and said, "We'll probably ride the four-wheeler for a bit in the field. Might pull James around in the old canoe for a bit. Then I think we might fish some in Mr. Gann's pond."

Uncle Trace finished chewing, took a sip of coffee, cleared his throat, and said, "Just remember what I said now. I don't want you boys near that old house or the pond in the woods over there. Alright?"

We both nodded.

I wanted to ask why, but the way Uncle Traced had said it, I chose not to.

Shortly after breakfast, we were out in the building gassing up the four-wheeler. We spent the next three hours riding around in the field and taking turns pulling each other in the canoe. It was an old boat that Uncle Trace had got from a buddy years ago. We fished out of it for a while until Uncle Trace got the Jon boat. By then the canoe had gotten a big hole near the back of it, so me and Matt had the idea of cutting the back half off and using it as a makeshift sled during the last great snowstorm we had two years ago. We talked Uncle Trace into doing it, and we played with that thing ever since. We didn't need no snowstorm. We just tied it up to the back of the four-wheeler and drug each around the field with it.

I remember it was my turn to ride, and Matt had been pulling me around the field for a few minutes when he returned to the muddy trail for a stretch. I watched as he stood up and peered out ahead like he saw something. He slowed to a stop.

"What is it?" I asked but he didn't answer.

He eased up a little bit then started looking at something on the ground next to him.

"What is it?" I said again.

He didn't say anything, but only pointed at the ground.

I rose from having my legs crossed Indian style in the canoe and strode over for a better look.

In the mud before us were two footprints. Each had four toes and were at least two maybe three times the size of my own foot when I placed my boot next to them. I remember the hairs on my neck standing up and a sliver of goosebumps spreading over my flesh. I gulped and looked at Matt who only stared with wide eyes, not saying a word.

I glanced around the field as I had the sudden feeling we were being watched. By who or what I had no idea, but I could feel their eyes glaring into my soul.

Finally, Matt said something. "Oh, it's probably just that half retarded man staying out there in that old house."

"Don't say that."

"Why? Are you half retarded or something?"

I snickered and said, "No, but I think you are."

He made a funny face and crossed his eyes at me.

I shook my head and squatted down for a better look of the prints.

"I'll bet it's the old man. I heard he looks like the giant off the Goonies. I'll just bet that ole sucker only has four toes. He probably comes out here butt naked at midnight and chases the deer around."

I chuckled and said, "Shut up. You're crazy, you know that?"

"I'll bet my right nut it's the truth."

"You keep betting like that and pretty soon you ain't going to have no nuts."

We both got the giggles at that.

We brushed off the footprints and went back to what we were doing. An hour later we were ready to go fishing, so we headed back to the house for a quick lunch before packing our gear.

We loaded our rods and tackle boxes onto the four-wheeler and strapped down a cooler full of diet Sundrop and Cheerwine like we were real rednecks ready to raise hell. They were diet because regular soda would raise Matt's sugar too much. We also had to pack plenty of snacks in case his sugar decided to go the opposite direction and leave him feeling like a sack of taters. I always knew when his sugar wasn't right because he'd start acting funny. If it was high, he'd get all hyper and start talking crazy like some crack head outside a convenient store late at night. If it was low, like I said, he'd go limp like a sack of taters. He'd start acting tired and sleepy, and I'd know he needed a snack or something sweet to give him for the boost he needed.

After packing the four-wheeler, we went into Uncle Trace's building in search of a can to put worms in. Matt found an old Folger's Coffee can that only had a few screws and bolts in it. He dumped it out, and off we went to the chicken pen. That was always the best place to dig for worms. They had about a dozen chickens of all different kinds. Everything from Road Island Reds, Domineckers, and whatever the solid white ones are called.

We gathered our worms and headed back to the four-wheeler. Matt crunk it up, and we were on our way. We trudged along the trail through the pines before coming out to the field. He followed the path along the wood line, and within ten minutes we were at Mr. Gann's pond.

Matt tied on his new black skirted spinner bait while I tried my luck with a white floating worm. Within half an hour we had both caught two pretty good size bass a piece. We spent another hour without either of us getting a bite.

"I might try catfishing for a bit," Matt said as he walked down the bank towards me.

"Yeah, I think I'll do the same."

We fished for another hour or so, waiting for a big cat to strike but that moment never came.

Me and Matt sat on the bank with our fishing rods resting in y shaped branches we had jammed into the dirt. Mr. Gann's house sat in the distance behind us up on the hill. We were in the middle of talking about the hottest girls at school when we heard the man's tractor rev up. We turned around to see him backing out from beneath the lean to next to his barn. He spotted us and tipped his straw hat. We both smiled and waved back.

"I've always liked old Mr. Gann. He's a good feller." Matt said. "He showed me and my dad his gun collection once after he'd invited us over for oyster stew. Whew. You wouldn't believe the kind of guns that man has."

"Really? Like what?"

"Shoot. He's got everything from Civil War muskets, to single shot rifles from World War One to Garands and Tommy Guns from the second World War. He has a whole room full of safes slap full of stuff."

"Wow, that's crazy."

"Yeah, it's wild. He promised to leave me and Dad a Garand and Wilson when he's gone. He also mentioned he'd leave us both a 1911 pistol."

"That's aweso—"

My words were cut short by the sound of something walking in the woods across the pond. Me and Matt both went silent and glared at the woods. Whatever it was, must've known we were watching because it never moved after that. I had the eerie feeling that even though I couldn't see it, it could see me. My mind flashed back to the footprints we found in the field.

"Aww it ain't nothing. Probably a deer." Matt said without much confidence in his voice.

"Right. Yeah, just a deer probably." I added while trying to sound tough.

"Fish ain't biting, you won't to call it day and head back before it gets much later?" Matt asks.

I nodded, "Yeah, sounds good."

We loaded up the four-wheeler and made it home just in time for supper. The whole ride back I struggled to rid the feeling we were being watched. I kept looking back behind us as I held onto the metal bars while Matt steered us home. I kept imagining something stepping out of the wood line and bolting after us. I told myself I had watched too many horror flicks and that things like that only happened in movies.

After supper, me and Matt went to Uncle Trace's building and dug out the tent. We made camp on the other side of the backyard fence. After setting the tent up, we gathered sticks and branches for our fire. Uncle Trace let us use some of the firewood he and Matt had stacked a week ago. We just needed some kindling to get things going. Aunt Amy gave us a bag of marshmallows.

As the sun set and darkness covered the earth, we found ourselves seated around the fire taking turns seeing who had the scariest ghost story.

I listened to Matt give his rendition of the man with a golden arm. He was in the middle of crying out in hoarse voice, "Where's my golden arm? Where's my golden arm?" when a branch snapped in the woods behind us. We both yelped and spun around.

The crickets got quiet and so did the cicadas singing from the trees. A gentle breeze whispered over the leaves. The clear sky gave way for the full moon's light. We stared at the wood line and did not dare make a sound. Slowly, the crickets and cicadas returned to their song. Me and Matt looked at each other for a moment. He smiled and said, "I'm telling you it's that crazy hermit that lives out there in Mr. Gann's old house. I heard he's even feral or something."

"But for real. What do you think those footprints belong to?"

"You mean *who* do they belong to? Not *what* do they belong to."

"You know what I meant."

"I don't know. That was weird. I mean who in the world would be out walking in a field barefoot like that?"

"Right. That's what I'm saying."

Matt tightened his lips and poked a stick around in the fire, sending embers heavenward.

"Dad's been acting kind of weird lately about not wanting us around that other pond. It's like he knows something."

I shifted on the log I was sitting on to give my left butt cheek a rest. I leaned forward and said, "What do you mean?"

"I don't know. It's just that over the last few weeks or so, he keeps pounding it into my brain not to go near that other pond and to stay away from the abandoned house."

"Do you think Mr. Gann may have told him to keep us away?"

Matt shrugged his shoulders, "Maybe. I don't know." He tossed the stick into the fire and stood to cross to the pile of logs. I watched him pick one up and place it on the fire as he said, "I kind of want to go over there to see what all the fuss is about."

"No. We can't do that. We'd get in trouble."

"Not if no one ever knew but us." Matt looked up at me and added, "I mean come on, how would anyone know if we never got caught?"

I looked down to find a rolly polly ambling around near my boot. I picked it up and watched it ball up in my palm.

Matt came over to me and took it out of my hand. He talked as he did so, "We sneak over there on the four-wheeler, have a quick look around, then head back the way we came." I watched as he took the last swig from his can of diet Sundrop before dropping the rolly polly inside.

"What are you doing?"

He didn't answer but just kept talking about the plot to sneak over to the pond. He placed the can at the side of the fire and squished it into the coals.

"There's a trail that goes in and out of there. We don't even have to go through the field. Less chance of being seen that way."

"How do you know about the trail?"

"I saw it with my dad one time when we were deer hunting out there. He warned me too not to go over there."

"I mean if he's warned you that much about it, there must be a good reason."

"Yeah, maybe that's where the old man stores his werewolf skins." Matt said and laughed.

"Like on that one Goosebumps episode?"

"Yeah, were the kid stays with his Aunt and Uncle and finds out they're werewolves."

Matt laughed, but I didn't.

"What are you doing with that can anyway?"

"You'll see. It should be about done."

Matt took hold of the top part of the can then dumped it out into his palm. A fried rolly polly tumbled out. Matt looked at me with a crooked grin before tossing the bug into his mouth. He pealed his lips back and made obnoxious crunching sounds as he stared at me with big, wild eyes.

"Hmm. Mmm. Nothing like a fresh fried rolly polly."

"You are a nut. You know that?"

We stayed up for another hour before our tired eyes betrayed us. After Matt peed on the fire, we crawled into the tent and snuggled into our sleeping bags.

I woke up in the middle of the night to the sound of crunching leaves. I jolted out of my bag and formed an L. Everything was still again. Other than Matt's snoring, it was eerily quiet. I listened for a good while, but never heard anything else move in the woods. The sounds of night returned, and I went back to sleep.

The next morning, we went inside and ate leftover bacon and eggs. Uncle Trace and Aunt Amy were still in the bed, so we did our best to be quiet. Being serious and quiet was hard for us because all we had to do was look at one another the wrong way and we'd enter a giggling fit. After a quick breakfast we went back outside and shot Matt's bow a few times. We practiced on a Styrofoam deer Uncle Trace had set up in the back yard. One of its antlers had fallen off to make it look like the dog from the Grinch.

After sending a dozen or more arrows down range, we grew bored and tried our luck at making a human sling shot. We took two big tree limbs, dropped them into holes we'd dug with Uncle Trace's posthole diggers, then took a bicycle inner tube and tied it on each pole. I think we may have gotten the idea from that Jackass show or something, but I can't rightly recall. We both tried it, but other than it giving us a good running start, neither of us took flight.

"You ready to go fishing?" I asked.

"Yeah. Let's go. I'm going to go tell Mom and Dad what we're doing. You can go ahead and gather some worms if you want to."

"Yeah, good idea. Do you remember what you did with the worm can?"

"Should be on the second shelf on the right in Dad's building."

"Cool."

I made my way into Uncle Trace's building and tried flicking a light on but had no luck. The bulb must've burned out or something. As I was combing through the darkness in search of the worm can I knocked something off a shelf. It fell onto the work bench with a loud clatter. It looked like a foot.

"What in the world?" I said as I leaned close for a better look.

It was a thick, white foot.

My eyes grew wide at the realization of what it was. I had seen one before on an episode of Monster Quest. It was a plaster cast of a footprint. It was way too big to be a man's. This thing would be almost twice the size of my dad's foot and he wore like a size twelve or something.

I heard Matt step inside as I turned the cast over in my hands and studied it.

"You find the worm can?" He called to me.

I answered with a question of my own.

"What the heck is this?"

I watched his jaw drop as he froze into place. He tried to say something but only stuttered.

"He must've hidden it behind something on the shelf. I knocked it down while looking for the worm can. Is this what I think it is?"

"Dude. No way."

"Maybe this is why your dad doesn't want us near that other pond."

"No. It's probably just something he bought off eBay. You know how he likes to buy odd things and antiques off there."

"But why was it hidden?"

"I don't know. Did you find the worm can?"

"Yeah, I got it right here."

"Alright, well let's get going. Dad said he might take us to the flea market later. And make sure you put that back where it was."

"Yeah, I'll try to."

I looked the cast over once more before returning it to the shelf. I thought about that thing the whole way to Mr. Gann's pond. Why did Uncle Trace have it in his building? Why was it hidden the way it was?

Matt parked the four-wheeler and hopped off.

"Hey, you alright? Space to ground patrol come in. Where you at dude?"

I shook my head and returned from my daze.

"Sorry, I was thinking."

Matt snickered and wagged his head, "I noticed."

I climbed off the wheeler and took up my fishing pole and tackle box.

"I can't stop thinking about your dad having that cast in his building like that. It's weird, isn't it?"

"Yeah, but so are your big ears."

"Oh hush. I'm being serious."

"Me too."

I punched his arm, and we made our way to the water's edge.

"What is it about that other pond? Is there something over there they don't want us to know about?" I said as I made a cast.

"Like what? A wild man with a big foot and humongous wiener?"

"I'm being for real. What if there's like a family of Sasquatches over there or something?"

"That'd be so cool. Like on Harry and the Henderson's?"

"Yeah. Something like that."

"Well let's head over and see then."

"What, right now?"

"Why not? You chicken?"

"No. I mean I just don't want to get in trouble that's all."

Matt hooked his spinner bait onto the middle eye of his rod and smiled, "How are we going to get in trouble if no one ever knows we're over there?"

I felt my heart pound hard behind my ribs as Matt drove the wheeler up and over a steep hill before aiming for the trail he'd talked about. In the far distance to my left, I could see the abandoned house sitting atop the hill. It glared down at us with its crooked shutters and flaking paint. I could see that part of the roof had caved in. There's no way anyone lived there. Matt had to just be pulling my leg. The house reminded me of something from the Chainsaw Massacre, and I half expected to see Leather Face himself come charging down the hill after us wielding a chain saw over his head. I shook the image away and tightened my grip on the metal bars. We disappeared into a thick grove of pines and snaked our way deeper into the woods. It got super dark as the sun was blocked out from all the growth. Pine needles littered our path as we crunched over pine combs and swatted away spider webs. Matt jerked the four-wheeler to a sudden halt and climbed off.

"What are you doing?" I asked as I watched him dart away as if searching for something.

He grabbed a branch and rushed back.

"This ought to do the trick." He said as he jammed the branch in place at the front of the four-wheeler. "You know how much I friggin hate spiders."

We continued onward. I had to adjust the fishing rods as my lure almost got caught on a limb. Matt hit a big stump that rattled us pretty good.

I heard him groan and grab his crotch, "Oh that didn't feel too good. I think I might be sterile for now on."

I laughed and shook my head.

As we traversed the narrow path, I kept my eyes peeled. I hadn't gotten the feeling of being watched yet, but the way this place looked, I knew it wouldn't be long before I did.

I could see the pond up ahead behind all the limbs. The trail finally opened up, and I watched a big Blue Heron walk along the bank before taking to the air. Matt turned the engine off in time to hear the Heron curse us out in that old grouchy voice they all have.

"Man. This place looks like paradise." Matt said with awe.

I was still skeptical. I kept turning around and checking over my shoulders to be sure nothing was creeping up behind us.

We grabbed our gear and headed down to the water's edge. There were a handful of dead trees standing around us. Matt made the comment that if the fish didn't bite at least we had plenty of trees to push over. That was something we enjoyed doing behind his house and we sometimes did it at Mr. Gann's pond if we got bored enough. We munched on granola bars and sipped on Capri Sun's that Matt had snuck along.

He couldn't have more than one or they'd jack his sugar up. I was careful to keep a watch on what he ate and drank because the last thing I wanted was to have to carry his butt back to the house after he'd entered a diabetic coma.

We finished off our snacks and placed our trash in a pile near a stump. We'd clean up when were done. That's one thing I can say about us is we always left where we fished the same way we found it. Of course, that probably had much to do with that time our dad's got ticketed by the Game Wardens in Chimney Rock. We got caught tossing an empty corn can and Vienna sausage can into the creek. That's a tale for another day though. The moral of the story is I guess we learned our lesson.

We spent a good hour walking the banks, fishing for bass. Other than a few good bites and something big that Matt missed, we didn't catch a darn thing. While I made my way to the corner of the pond where a small stream filtered in, I noticed something in the mud along the bank. As I came closer, I could tell it was footprints. At first, I thought maybe Matt had wandered over here when I wasn't looking and had made the tracks, but when I looked closely, I noticed I didn't see any shoe tread. That's when I saw the toes. All four of them. The footprints meandered along before trudging out into the water and disappearing. Now mind you this is early fall, so the first thought that entered my mind was *Why in the world would someone be wandering around barefoot out here?* The second thought was, *Who the heck goes swimming in a pond when it's barely sixty degrees outside?*

I hollered at Matt and had him come take a look. He made another joke about the old man living in the abandoned house.

"I don't think no one lives up there. Did you not see how run down that place is?"

"No, not really. I was too busy driving I guess."

"These tracks are weird." I said as I retrieved my phone and snapped some pictures.

We had no luck in bass fishing, so as usual, we resorted to catfishing. I caught a bream, and we shared it for cut bait.

After clipping some bobbers between the eyes of our rods like the old carp fishermen do to know when they get a bite, and situating our rods in the crevice of Y branches, Matt said, "You want to push down some trees while we wait?"

I smiled and said, "Does a bear crap in the woods?"

We walked back up the bank towards the patch of dead pin oaks. I went one way and Matt went another. I found one I thought I could handle and gave it a good shake, keeping a check on the top of course. After a few good shoves it gave way, and I yelled out, "Timber!"

Matt cheered me on as he worked one of his own. I turned my back and went searching for another. I heard the tree crack and then heard Matt screaming for his life. When I turned around, I saw him high stepping through the woods as the big tree fell after him. It bit at his heels before slamming into the ground and breaking into pieces. How he managed to have that thing chase after him that way sure beats the hell out of me. How he outran it is even crazier. He was laughing and screaming like a caveman after having downed a buffalo.

I shook my head and couldn't help but laugh with him.

My laughing stopped at the sound of something grunting from the gulley next to me. I froze in place except for turning my head to look down at where the sound came from. Thick kudzu was spread out everywhere and it must've been a good twenty foot drop off the embankment. I heard movement below me. My pulse quickened and my mouth went dry. A horrible stench wafted into the air. It reminded me of a wet dog after it had just finished rolling in a cow patty. I began to gag.

Whatever was moving around in the kudzu let out a deep and guttural growl. The sound echoed among the pines. Matt stopped laughing. I turned and looked at him. He was like a statue and only stared at me with wide eyes. I motioned with my hand for him to crank the four-wheeler. I watched as he began taking calculated steps towards the ATV.

There was more movement down the hill. Whatever it was, was heavy. I could distinguish the sound of two big feet thumping onto the forest floor. My mind shot back to the tracks in the pond. I could visualize something big and hairy walking out into the pond for an evening swim. That's probably why it stunk so bad. All that algae and crap had dried onto its fur.

It growled again and every hair on my body stood straight. That's when it bolted up the hill after me. It thrashed through the thicket and was racing towards me faster than I could blink. I made a break for the four-wheeler and heard Matt trying to crank it. The stupid thing sputtered and acted like it wanted to leave us for dead, but as I pounded closer it came to life. I could hear the monster grunting and tearing through the woods after me.

"C'mon! Hurry!" Matt screamed.

He stretched out his hand. I grabbed it and he helped sling me onto the seat behind him. He was already giving the wheeler gas before I was completely on board. I didn't dare look back because all I could imagine seeing was a huge, clawed hand reaching for my jugular. I wrapped my arms around Matt's waist and held on for dear life as he high tailed it out of there. One of my extra rods I'd brought along got its lure snagged in a tree limb. It peeled drag for a good twenty yards before snapping off. I didn't care. A lost fishing lure was the least of my worries at that point. A long trail of line flapped in the wind behind us as Matt aimed for the field. As creepy as that field always was, I'd never longed so much to be back. Anywhere but here in the thick pines with some angry beast thrashing after us.

We finally entered the clearing and Matt shifted into high gear as we bolted towards the hill where the house was instead of traveling along the trail near the wood line. It wasn't until we reached the top of the hill that I finally looked behind us. I patted Matt's gut and yelled for him to stop.

"What? Are you crazy?"

"No, it's alright. Stop for a second."

He did.

Down the hill from where we had just come, a large pine tree swayed side to side as if being shaken by a giant. Was it imitating what we were doing earlier?

"What in the world?" Matt said.

"Alright, that's enough. Let's get home."

He turned around and pushed us onward.

Uncle Trace was about to light a brush pile on fire when we came racing out of the woods to the backyard. Uncle Trace rose from flicking a lighter and looked at us with a hand shielding the sun.

He chuckled when he saw the fishing line trailing behind us. "Yeah, y'all got spooked didn't ya?"

We were both gasping for breath by that point and had trouble describing what had just happened.

"Slow down now. Are you hurt anywhere? Are you both alright?"

We nodded.

"Something...chase...chased us." Matt managed.

The smile disappeared from Uncle Trace's face.

"Matthew. Did you go to the other pond?"

Neither of us said anything.

Uncle Trace clenched his teeth and shook his head, "Boy, I told you not to go down there. Didn't I?"

"Yes sir."

"What happened?"

We did our best to recount the events, but of course it didn't sound as good out loud. You just had to be there to understand it all.

Uncle Trace listened carefully and studied us both with prying eyes. He scratched the back of his neck and said, "I don't want you going in the woods anymore without me." He looked up at us and added, "Is that understood?"

"Yes sir." We said together.

It got quiet among us as Uncle Trace seemed to consider whether he should tell us something or not.

"What is it, Uncle Trace?" I asked.

He swallowed and bit the inside of his jaw. He glanced around to be sure Aunt Amy wasn't listening.

He bent over and placed his hands to his knees. He motioned for us to come closer.

"Come here. This stays between us, okay?"

We both nodded.

"Mr. Gann told me something the other night. I haven't told anyone because I thought he was just pulling my leg like he likes to do. Plus, I think he may have had a little too much to drink. Anyway. Mr. Gann said he saw something the other day when he was cleaning up around the old house."

"You mean the abandoned house that belonged to his parents?" I asked.

Uncle Trace bobbed his head and said, "Yeah. He said he heard something scream down by that pond. When he looked up, he saw a pine tree swaying the way y'all did. Then he said he got to looking and could see something squatted near the wood line watching him. Said he thought it was a bear at first because of how big and dark it was. But he said he knew it wasn't a bear because it stood up and walked on two legs for a good thirty yards before disappearing into the woods. Now he said the whole time he was watching this thing, that pine tree kept swaying."

"There's more than one." Matt said with wonder.

"Exactly."

Uncle Trace's words hung in the air for a moment before he added, "So. That said. I don't want you in the woods anymore without me, okay?"

He didn't have to say it twice. The message was delivered and received.

"And let's keep this between us like I said, alright?"

That was some twenty years ago, and until now, I've kept that promise. The only reason I decided to write this story was because I wanted my kids and grandkids to be able to read it one day. Ever since that day by the pond I've been hesitant about venturing too far into the woods. Nowadays, I never go past the wood line without a gun. If you'd encountered what me and my cousin did that day, I think you'd probably be the same way. You just never know what's lurking in the woods with you.

I know some people who think the woods are like a Disney cartoon, full of Bambi's and Thumpers. I'm not that naïve because I know without a shadow of a doubt . . . somethings out there.

The Tony Hole

I heard the thumb latch click on the front door.

The door jimmied a bit before someone started knocking. Our three yorkies, Peanut, Britney, and Kayley yapped and jolted from my parents' room. I could hear their toenails clicking on the hardwood before they stopped at the top of the staircase. The knocking came again. I rose from bed and rubbed my eyes. I could hear my mom and dad talking as my dad marched down the steps to the door. By now, I was coming down the hall. I found my mom standing at the top of the stairs tying a knot in her robe. She glared down at the door. I went and stood next to her and followed her gaze. I saw the hulking back of my father as he unlocked the door. My brother was on the other side and gasped for breath. His girlfriend, Danielle, cried into her hands. Her brother, Chad, who was a good friend of my brother, walked in circles with his hands to his head.

"What's wrong? What happened?" My dad asked. As he stepped outside.

My mom called out as she made her way down the steps, "What's going on, Will?"

She cracked the door and listened. I stood tight against her and eaves dropped.

I'd never heard my brother that frightened before. I knew something bad must've happened, but I had no idea what.

"We. We were waiting for the the dogs down near the Tony Hole. It sounded like they were right next to it. So, we drove over there and . . ." He trailed off and swallowed hard to find the words.

"And? Is everyone alright?" My dad asked.

My brother nodded and continued.

"We pulled up and cut the truck off to listen. We sat there for a while and didn't hear the dogs no more, so I crunk the truck back up and started to back out of there when Daniele and Chad started screaming. I turned around and that's when I saw him."

"Saw who?"

"Tony."

I remember a chill running over my spine when he said his name. My whole life I had heard stories of why everyone on our road calls that one spot at the creek, The Tony Hole. You had to go down a long side trail that followed the perimeter of Old Man Dixon's cornfield before reaching the back where Crowder's Creek ran. You would then have to follow a narrow path through the woods that came out at a set of three dilapidated, log cabins. The cabins supposedly belonged to Old Man Dixon's great grandfather and was used to house his slaves. He had given them each a share of the profits from the harvest along with an acre of land, shelter, and a decent wage. The slaves respected and loved Harvey Dixon as he treated them all as family and all he asked in return was for them to help him and his sons with preparing the harvest with which he ran the family business. One slave in particular, Harvey Dixon regarded as his own son. The man's name was Tony Dye. When Harvey Dixon fell ill and his two sons decided to start their own ventures outside of the family business, it was Tony Dye who Harvey left in charge of the farm. Harvey Dixon granted another ten acres along with forty percent of the business to Tony as long as he promised to take care of things when Harvey passed. Tony agreed.

A few months later, as Harvey Dixon lay dying in bed, Tony and his sons were catfishing late one night at the creek next to the cabins where they lived. With Harvey's son's becoming envious of Tony upon learning of their father's wishes, the two men decided to teach Tony a lesson. The two Dixon brothers sneaked up on Tony and his sons and overtook the man. As one brother held Tony's arms, the other pummeled his face and gut. Tony broke away at one point and got in two good licks on one of the brothers before the other kicked him from behind and sent him sprawling into the creek. Having just taken a beating and never learning to swim, Tony quickly succumbed to the current. His body was discovered the next day, floating face down along the creek bank.

My brother's story pulled me back to the present.

"I saw him standing in the headlights, dressed in a white baggy shirt and fishing jeans rolled at the cuff with holes in them. He stared at us. Then the lights went out on my truck. The battery was dead. I tried cranking it, but it wouldn't even try. I got out with my light and gun and stepped in front of the truck. Danielle and Chad were screaming for me to get back inside, but something in me just had to see if it was really him. It was like I was being drawn by something. I couldn't help it. I just had to see."

I gripped tighter to my mama and listened.

"As I walked through the field toward the creek bank, a gust of wind picked up and all the reeds bent over like they were bowing to something."

My brother shut his eyes and scratched the back of his neck before continuing, "I had an eerie feeling turn in my gut. I felt like I was being watched or something. I don't know how else to explain it. I kept walking closer to the water's edge. I reached the top of the bank and shined my light down at the water . . ."

He trailed off again and drew a deep breath.

"What did you see?" My dad asked.

"It was a body."

My mom gasped.

"What?" My dad said.

My brother nodded, "They were wearing a baggy white shirt like the slaves wore. It looked like a black man. He was floating face down with his arms spread out. I only got to see it for a few seconds because my light went dead like my truck. I turned and bolted out of there. Danielle and Chad had the truck locked when I got back. I hopped in and tried the ignition again. It crunk right up like nothing had ever happened. We peeled out and headed this way. I even left my coon dogs down there."

Things got quiet for a moment as everyone was deep in thought. I could hear cicadas singing from the trees and tree frogs screeching from the woods.

My dad cleared his throat and said, "And you're sure that's what you saw?"

My brother stared at the ground with wide eyes as he nodded and said, "I know for a fact I saw a body down there." He looked up at Danielle and Chad and said, "We all saw him standing there in the head lights."

"Do you think we should go back to check on things? Make sure they ain't no one down there in need of help. You probably need to get your dogs anyway."

"Are you sure that's a good idea, Will? Shouldn't you just call the sheriff instead?" My mom asked.

Chad spoke for the first time and said, "I'm not going back there. Huh uh. No way man. You can forget it."

"Me either. I'll never go back there." Danielle added.

"We'll be fine honey. I don't want to involve the sheriff unless we have to," Dad turned back around and said to Danielle and Chad, "Alright, well we can take you two home before we go." He looked to my brother and added, "Johnathan, you want to drop them off and meet me at Old Man Dixon's?"

"Yeah. Bring some extra lights with you and be sure to bring your gun too."

"Alright, well give me time to get dressed, and I'll meet you over there in about half an hour."

As my dad stepped back inside, I began to plead with him. "Can I go with you? Please? Please? I want to go."

He looked at mom.

"Not without me you're not." She said.

It was just after midnight when my parents and I backed up our driveway in Dad's old dodge pickup to head for the Tony Hole. I rode in between them on the bench seat. We bypassed Old Man Dixon's driveway and angled for the long dirt road about fifty yards past his house.

We found my brother waiting there in his truck. We followed him as the road led to Old Man Dixon's hundred-acre cornfield. If you continued following it, it would lead you to the back of the field where the crop turned to woods next to the creek bank. We eased our way along the narrow road by the cornfield. The cab of the truck bounced as we ran over roots and potholes. A light mist began to descend. Dad's wiper blades screeched as they swiped the droplets aside. Dad had the windows cracked slightly, and I could hear the cicadas screeching. A hoot owl called out nearby. I watched my brother apply his brakes as we reached the place where he said he saw Tony. Dad put the truck in park and killed the engine. He stepped out and shut the door. He spoke through the cracked window, "Stay here with your mama, Son."

"You're not leaving us here." My mama said as she opened the truck door. I slid over and hopped out with her.

Dad sighed and clicked on his flashlight. I saw he had his pistol holstered on his hip.

"So, this is where you first saw him?" My dad asked my brother.

I watched Johnathan shut his door and click on a light of his own, "Yeah. Right over there." He pointed the light over a patch of old reeds near the wood line. A narrow deer trail cut through the middle of them.

I clung tight to my mama as we followed my dad and brother along the path. A briar struck me on the arm. Another poked my cheek. Something rustled in the woods. I yelped and squeezed my mama's arm so hard she cried out, "Ow! Cameron, let go. You're hurting me."

We regrouped and continued onward. I kept looking behind us as the feeling of an approaching monster loomed in my mind. If I stared into the darkened wood line long enough, I could almost make out a big hairy beast with dripping wet fangs and glowing red eyes. I jerk my eyes away and refocused on the trail ahead.

A pack of coyotes bellowed in the distance. I heard something move in the brush next to us. My dad and brother jerked their light to the sound. I heard dad unholster his pistol. We stood still for a moment and listened. A soft breeze whispered among the reeds and sent them bowing like my brother had described. I gulped and wiped at the sweat forming on my brow. I licked my lips and tasted something salty and copper. The wind ceased and all went still.

We moved again and continued towards the creek. I began to hear water rippling over the rocks as we neared the edge of the bank. We stood along the edge and watched as my dad and brother shined their lights down at the creek.

"I know I saw him floating right there. It was plain as day. He was right there. I promise you."

My dad walked further up the creek and swiped his light this way and that. My brother went the other way. My mama and me stood in the middle and took turns glancing at the end of their lights beam. Satisfied there weren't any bodies floating along the creek bank, they came back towards us. As they were nearing, a branch snapped across the creek. Both of their lights jerked in that direction. In what couldn't have been more than two seconds before the light went out, a family of five dressed in white gowns stood there staring at us. My mama let out a sound I had never heard her make before. The instant the lights went out, we all bolted back for the trucks.

I remember the truck fishtailing as the tires finally grabbed asphalt. My brother was right behind us.

We didn't talk about what we saw until the next day. Which happened to fall on a Saturday, so my brother and my parents were all home from school and work. My brother had set his mind on going back there with a snorkel and goggles to see for himself if anything was in the creek. My parents protested his idea of course, but eventually, curiosity got the best of my dad, and he was able to convince my mom to agree to it. So, that morning around ten or so we all headed back to the Tony Hole. I rode with my brother this time as Mom and Dad followed.

My brother had his radio tuned to a classic country station and Merle Haggard sang *Mama Tried.* We had the windows rolled down in his Ford Ranger and the cab bounced as we jostled our way along the trail next to Old Man Dixon's field.

I caught a glimpse of my brother's hand as he reached to turn down the volume.

"What's got you so quiet over there, huh? Still thinking about last night?"

The truth was, I had never stopped thinking about it. I couldn't have slept for maybe an hour or two at the most. Even when I did drift off, I only dreamed of the people we saw across the creek. They were the same people I had been secretly drawing pictures of for the past six months after they started visiting my window at night.

I turned and looked at my brother, debating whether I should tell him or not.

"What's the matter?"

I swallowed hard before reaching into my back pocket. I took out a folded piece of paper and held it on each end to stretch it tight.

"What is this?"

"Just look at it."

"I am. It looks like the people from last night. You done good."

"I drew that last week."

I felt him apply the brakes.

"You did what now?"

"I said I drew this last week. I have a stack tucked away in my closet. I started last fall."

My brother started laughing and shook his head, "Oh, you had me going for a minute there, Cam. You really did."

I folded the paper and tucked it back in my pocket.

"It started with a tap on my window."

My brother stopped laughing. He cleared his throat and listened.

"I would hear it almost every night. Sometimes it'd wake me up at like two or three in the morning. Other times I was too sleepy to look. After a few weeks went by of it tapping on the glass, I started hearing whispers. I could never see where they came from, but I could hear them plain as day."

With his voice sticking to his throat he asked, "What did they say?"

"My name. They would say my name and then ask me to open the window."

"Alright, now you're starting to creep me out a little bit."

I kept going, "A few weeks after the whispers, I woke up late one night to find two of them standing outside the window. They were smiling at me."

"Shit, are you serious? Sorry, I didn't mean to cuss."

"It's alright. Yeah, I don't think this just started though."

"What do you mean?"

"I've always had a weird feeling in our house. I mean, you remember I didn't start sleeping in my own bed until I was like what seven or eight?"

"Yeah, I thought you were going to sleep on that cot next to Mom and Dad until your legs were hanging over the end of it."

"Oh, shut up." I said as I punched his arm.

"Ow, you frogged me."

"I'm being serious though. I've always felt something in our house. And do you remember my imaginary friend I used to have?"

I watched my brother give it some thought.

"Yeah. What did you call him? Tommy wasn't?"

I nodded, "I've been thinking though."

"Yeah, what's that?"

"That's awfully close to Tony, isn't it?"

Johnathan snapped his head at me, "No. You don't really think so, do you?"

"I always said he was a grown up."

"So, you're saying this whole time your imaginary friend was really Tony Dye?"

I shrug my shoulders, "I'm just saying."

My brother cursed again and apologized.

We reached the back of the field, and he eased the truck to a halt. My parents parked next to us.

I looked at my brother and said, "Do me a favor will ya?"

"What's that?"

"Don't tell them what I just told you, okay?"

"As long as you don't tell them I cussed around you."

"Deal."

We shook on it and climbed out of the truck. My brother grabbed a black duffle bag from the bed and walked towards the embankment.

"Did you make sure to get the rope from the building like I said?" My dad asked him.

"Yeah, it's in here." My brother said while shouldering the bag.

"Here take this." I watched as my dad passed him a flashlight.

My mom spoke up, "I don't know about this, y'all. What if you get caught in the current? Then what?"

"Well, that's what the rope's for. We'll tie it into a harness around him like they use in the army when they repel down a building. I'll wrap it around this tree and hold on to it down by the bank."

"I'll be fine, Mom. I'll be careful. I just want to look around and see what's down there."

Moments later my dad was fitting the rope around him, and he was wading into the current. I sat next to my dad and watched as he intertwined his wrist in the rope. My brother descended to about waist deep and turned to look at us through his goggles and snorkel. He gave the okay sign and sunk beneath the surface.

I heard my mom mumble from the top of the bank as we watched bubbles spread across the water's surface. He was down there for about thirty seconds before resurfacing.

"Anything?" I asked.

He shook his head and smacked the flashlight.

"It's darker than I thought down there. Even the light doesn't help much."

He took a deep breath and tried again.

He stayed down longer this time. A second set of bubbles surfaced.

"Will, is he alright?"

No sooner than my mom's words filled the air, the rope jerked. It caught Dad by surprise and tugged him forward.

"What the hell?" I heard him mutter under his breath as he regripped the rope.

My mama began screaming, "Pull him up, Will. Oh my God! PULL HIM UP!"

More bubbles popped at the surface. The rope yanked again. My dad started pulling. I joined in behind him and did the same.

A big patch of bubbles came up and the water began to swirl.

"Here he is." My dad said with a smile in his tone.

I watched as Johnathan broke the surface and gasped for air.

Mama raced down the embankment and nearly tripped trying to get to him. He peeled the goggles off and tossed the snorkel.

"What happened down there?" My dad asked as he stood and wandered to the water's edge to be next to my mama.

My brother coughed and hacked as he waded closer. I noticed something in his right hand but couldn't yet make out what it was.

"I swear I saw a hand down there."

"A hand?" My dad questioned.

"Yeah. I saw it out of the corner of my eye. It was gone when I turned to look, but I found these on the bottom next to a stump."

They jingled when he held them up. It was a ring of keys. They looked old.

"What in the world?" Dad questioned as he reached out to study them.

I nudged closer for a better look. As I strained and watched Dad wipe muddy silt off them, it hit me. I looked at Johnathan and said, "The box."

"Huh?"

I felt everyone's eyes on me at once.

"The box. You know. The one me and Josh found last summer buried behind the cabin."

I saw my brother's eyes light up at my words. "The one we could never open because there was no key."

I nodded and bounded on my feet, "Yeah, the one we kept saying looked like it could belong to the civil war days."

"Do you think these would work it?" Johnathan asked.

"Only one way to find out." Said my dad.

WE GOT BACK to the house, and I rushed to rummage my closet for the box. I knelt on my knees and snatched at anything and everything that wasn't the box, tossing it out onto the floor behind me.

"Boy, you keep going like that and you'll have a mess to clean up when you're done." Said Dad.

"Yeah, and you better not hide it all under the bed like you did last time." Mama added.

I heard the keys jangle behind me as my brother spun them around on his finger.

"Ah ha. Got it." I said as I swiped away the winter coat it was buried under.

It was a rusted and earth warn piece of steal that must've weighed twenty pounds or more. I rolled it onto my lap and turned to my brother, stretching forth my hand. He passed me the keys.

"Here, let's bring it into the kitchen for a minute. Probably could use some WD-40 anyhow." Dad said as he relieved me of the box.

We followed him into the kitchen where Mom laid down a wash towel for the box to rest on.

Dad searched beneath the sink and rose with a can of oil. I watched as he extended the red straw and doused the keyhole.

"Alright. That ought to do the trick. Give it a go."

I slipped the first of about a dozen keys into the slot and wiggled. I tightened my lips and shook my head. I tried the next one. Nothing. It wasn't until about the eighth or ninth key that I felt some traction. A grin stretched my face, and I turned to look at everyone.

"Well don't just stand there. Crack that baby open." My brother said as he nudged me on the arm.

I gave the key another turn and could hear the gears click within. The door popped forward to reveal a slight crack. A musty, earthen odor flooded forth. I squinted and pulled on the door.

A small wicker basket sat in the center and a cloth bag rested in it with the top tied closed with a piece of twine. I wrinkled my brow and looked at my brother. He nodded at me. I returned my eyes to the bag and pulled it out to sit it on the towel next to the box. I slowly undid the twine. I could feel my heart palpitate with heightened anticipation. Sweat beaded on my forehead. I swallowed a gulp and dumped the contents of the bag onto the towel. A stack of black and white photos, which were clumped together, tumbled to the right and a wedding band with a string and note attached went to the left.

Dad leaned close and mumbled, "What in the world?"

Mom picked up the wedding band and said, "It's definitely a lady's ring. Too small for a man."

"What does the note say?" My brother asked.

We watched as she uncreased it and began to read, "To whomever fins this here ring, know that it once fitted the love of my life. She has since passed on to the great unknown, yet her spirit lives. My wish would be that should this ring ever be taken from this here box that whoever find the ring bury it beneath the shade of the large oak down by the creek's edge. My love's wish was for the ring to remain with me until my passing. My wish was to bury it with her, but that was not as she had wanted. Upon my death, I ask that this ring be buried where she lies beneath the oak. Her marker is there and there she is also. As we were joined on this earth so shall we be joined in heaven. Our spirits will not find rest until the deed is done."

Mom finished and folded the note back the way it was. Dad picked up the photos and began peeling them apart. I saw his eyes widen as he looked through them.

"What is it?" I asked.

I saw his Adam's Apple bob as he lowered the pictures for us all to see. It was family photos of the five we saw last night. The same five I've seen standing outside my window. It was Tony Dye and his family.

My brother cursed and we all jerked our heads to him.

"Sorry." He said as he shrugged.

A half hour later we were back at the Tony Hole searching for the tall oak by the creek bank. We counted four in total, picked the biggest of the bunch and began sifting the ground for a burial marker.

Mom called out to us, "Hey, I think I have something."

We crowded around her and watched as she swiped away leaves and loose dirt. A small rectangle piece of metal was planted at the base of the tree. I squatted down and wiped the dirt away with my thumb. I grabbed the bottom of my shirt, spit, and scrubbed at the placard.

"What does it say?" Mom asked.

"I can't really make it out much, but it looks like the last name is Dixon."

"Really? Dixon . . . why would she have the Dixon name?" My brother questioned.

"It wasn't uncommon for slaves to take the last name of their owner back then." Dad said.

Mom added, "Yeah, he's right. If Tony was as close to the man as they say, he probably eventually took on the last name. They say he was like a son to the old man."

I continued shining the marker until I could read the rest of it.

"Abigail Dixon Birth 1837 Death 1863."

"That's her. That's Tony's wife. Has to be." My brother said.

I looked up at Mom and said, "Do you have the ring?"

She nodded.

Later that night as I lay on my back with my hands behind my head, I thought about the past two days and the months leading up to them. I thought of all the dreams I'd had and the pictures I'd drawn. I remembered all the nightly visits. None of it started until me and my friend, Josh, found that box last fall. After it was taken was when things started. I'd always thought the story behind the Tony Hole was just an old tale all the parents liked to spook the kids and teenagers with. I figured it was just another piece of folklore like kids in England had of the Headless Horseman, or how my parents and their parents before them grew up with the ghost story of Crybaby bridge. I think every small town across America has a place called Crybaby bridge. I know we sure do.

After dazing at the ceiling and watching my ceiling fan make its revolutions, I eventually drifted to sleep sometime after midnight. I was awoken a short while later to the sound of tapping. I woke facing my window. Something I never do. I always turn my back to it, but I guess I must've rolled over in my sleep. I lifted my heavy lids and took a sledgehammer to my heart at the sight before me. I bolted upright and pulled the covers close to my face.

Standing at the other side of the window was Tony and his family. The initial fright slowly dissipated as a soothing calmness filled my heart. I watched as Tony stood with one arm around his wife, Abigail, and his other dangled around his three small children. They smiled at me, and for the first time since this all started, I truly knew they meant me no harm. I could just feel it in my gut. Fear washed from my heart. The youngest of the children raised a hand and waved. I waved back. I locked eyes with Tony for a moment. He smiled and nodded. I returned the gesture and watched as they turned and headed for the wood line before disappearing beneath the light of the moon.

Thank you for reading *Whispering Winds!* I hope you enjoyed it as much as I did writing it! If so, I would be grateful if you'd be kind enough to leave a review on Amazon as reviews truly are the life blood of any Author's career.

About the Author

I am a former college baseball player turned writer who thoroughly enjoys the outdoors, whether it be fishing, kayaking, hiking, and exploring new places, or watching a game of America's greatest pastime. I'm an old soul at heart, so I love old music (especially classic rock from CCR, Bob Seger, Bruce Springsteen, or vintage rock and roll from Chuck Berry, Muddy Water's, Elvis, etc) old movies and antique items. I own a Victrola Turntable in case you're not getting the picture yet.

I'm an avid reader and writer of Mystery, Horror, and Suspense. I enjoy reading Stephen King, Ted Dekker, Frank Peretti, Thomas Harris, Steven James, C.J. Box, and James Lee Burke to name a few. I also enjoy a fun/inspiring Southern Story as well such as Where the Crawdads Sing.

I was a top ten finalist in Inkshares 2018 Mystery/Thriller contest. I am a member of the Horror Writers Association. I hold an MBA from Coastal Carolina University and am currently practicing real estate in Myrtle Beach. You can find me on Instagram, Facebook, and YouTube to stay up to date with my latest work.

Instagram: randall_lane31
Facebook: Randall Lane Fiction
YouTube: Randall Lane Fiction
Amazon: Randall Lane Fiction

Other Books Available

If you enjoyed *Whispering Winds* then you'll likely enjoy my latest novel *The Reaping* as well. Available on Amazon! The book trailer is posted to my YouTube channel.

Synopsis: Something strange is happening in New England. Over the past 17 years, numerous children have disappeared after each of their parents were discovered brutally murdered and left with taunting notes. With rumors of the man in a black hood who roams the woods at night, to an escaped mental patient from Cushing Island, and a snake handling church with a dark past, veteran Homicide Detective, Laurie Daniels must work through this high stakes enigma to learn who the ghost-like killer really is. The deeper she goes the more she begins to believe the killer may be connected to her past. And a new, horrifying clue emerges . . . Daniels isn't closing in on the killer, but he's closing in on her. Can she catch him before he catches her?

Devil's Den is also available on Amazon. You can check out the book trailer for all my stories on the YouTube Channel.

Synopsis: The year is 1989 and as Detectives search for a local serial killer, James and Rebecca Randolph can't help but wonder if it may be Ethan, the new co-worker of James. After causing a horrendous accident at the Georgetown International Paper Mill, Ethan vanishes before further questioning. Locals are quick to term him the GTK or Georgetown Killer. 25 years later, after relocating to Holden Beach, James and Rebecca find themselves once again in the cross hairs of the GTK. As they consult the spiritual guidance of Native American

Friends, they soon learn there is a lot more going on than meets the eye. Embarking on a Journey from Darkness to Light, passing through the Devil's Den along the way, they gain a whole new perspective of the saying, "Good vs Evil."

I also have my novel *Omah*, available on Amazon too! To watch the book trailer, head over to my YouTube channel. (Randall Lane Fiction.)

Synopsis: After a string of mysterious disappearances and encounters in Northern California, Game Wardens are less than surprised when six-year-old Tyler Jacob's vanishes by the South Fork Eel River while fishing with his family. As the family is riddled with guilt and on the verge of losing hope, Native Americans from the local Yurok Tribe step in to help spread light on the recent events. While pushing through the vast wilderness and majestic Redwood Forest in search of his son, Randy Jacob's soon learns that what he once thought was just a Legend may actually be a living and breathing creature after all. As hours stretch into days and the clock rushes forward, can Tyler be found before it's too late?

Whispering Winds

Inside Look at Chapter 1

of Randall's next Novel

OLD
GHOSTS
OF THE
VALLEY

A NOVEL

RANDALL LANE

1

Chapel Valley, NC

October 2023

3:33 p.m.

Carol Gore is a fifty-nine-year-old divorced mother of two, who lives alone up in the backcountry of the Blue Ridge Mountains. She has lived in the same house since the early nineties. She and her husband, Steve, moved to the area after he'd picked up a mining job in the town of Chapel Valley. It was also around this time that Carol learned of the Abbott cult. A co-worker from Piggly Wiggly wouldn't shut up about the sweet little Abbott family and its parishioners, so Carol finally relented and accompanied her to an event at the compound. That was all it took for Carol to become hooked.

As Carol thinks back to the moment she first stepped foot on the Abbott compound, she subconsciously rinses off a few glass plates from previous days meals. Skylar, her white Himalayan cat, is busy weaving in and out between her feet. The tickle brings her back just in time to hear the strange noise. Carol thought she'd heard something earlier but only brushed it off as a play upon her ears. Must be the house settling or something, she'd said to herself. Isn't that what we always say? Or at least what we always hope for, right? What if we're wrong though? What if we're not alone during all the times we think we are? What if someone or something . . . lurks within the shadows and watches without our knowing?

As Carol asks herself these questions, she hears it again. The sound is unmistakable this time. The creaking of a floorboard beneath a sturdy, unwelcomed foot. All day she had fought the eerie feeling of being watched. It seems a presence had been hovering just over her shoulder. She's being too paranoid, she'd thought. Things are different now. To think she's still being watched . . . well it'll just end up driving her crazy. She can't allow herself to go on thinking this way. They would end up throwing her away to the place where people drift along in white gowns, while being force fed medicine and whipped into submission. She'll never go back there. She'd made a promise to herself, and she's determined within her heart to keep it.

No amount of self-encouragement can eat away the growing feeling she has of being watched. It is stronger now than ever before. The home is quiet other than the running of the faucet, and the black and white film playing in the living room. Carol stands frozen with her back to the rest of the kitchen. She looks down to find Skylar staring behind her. Together they listen.

Creeeaaak!

Skylar hisses and enters in a low crouch, his ears flare backward, his hair stands straight. Carol feels someone in the room. She turns just enough, so she can scan the room with her peripheral. She goes over the China cabinet full of Grandma's dishes and scans over the kitchen table. Her heart leaps at the big shadow of a man standing in the kitchen's door frame. She gasps and drops a dish. The crash of the shattering glass fills the room. She fights the urge to look directly at the man, knowing that the chance of her survival will quickly diminish should she see his face.

Skylar emits a low growl and backs up to be between Carol and the sink cabinet.

"What do you want?" Carol asks with her words sticking to her throat.

A moment passes.

"You."

Creeeeaaaaak!

The dark man takes a step.

"Stop. Don't come any closer."

He stops.

She grips the sinks hard enough to hurt her fingers.

"Look at me."

She shakes her head.

"Carol."

Her heart sinks at the knowledge of this mystery man knowing her name.

"Carol. You have to look at me. It's very important."

She clamps her eyes shut and shakes her head again.

She hears him breathe deep. He holds it, then sighs.

"I don't want to do this Carol, but I'm afraid I have to. You're leaving me no—"

Carol snatches Skylar up and bolts through the side door of the kitchen for her bedroom. Heavy thuds pound towards her. She slams the door shut and engages the lock. She rushes to move a chest of drawers against the door.

The dark man slams against the door as soon as Carol slides the furniture into place. The door rattles hard on its hinges. She stumbles backwards with one hand to her mouth, and the other reaching blindly for the bed.

Her heart will surely explode any moment as adrenaline courses through her veins in an icy rush. Her legs meet the edge of the bed, and she bruises a heel against the metal railing below. She winces and bends to tend to the pain.

The door rattles hard once more. Skylar growls again before going into a frantic search for cover. Another hard thud pounds against the door.

As Carol rubs her heel, she begins to hear a faint but hoarse whisper coming from under the bed. The scratchy voice stalls her racing heart and sends her body freezing in place. Movement comes from beneath the bed. It sounds like something crawling across the hardwood floor. Carol jerks herself up and looks toward the window. A sudden thought hits her. What an idiot. Last week she'd nailed the windows shut after fearing someone was secretly entering in the night. In her efforts to keep someone out, she ends up trapping herself in. She must break it. She races over to a nightstand and begins to search for something to break the glass.

The whisper under the bed becomes more audible now. Between the thuds against the door, she can make out the words. It's saying, "Come near my dear."

Carol yanks open a drawer to her nightstand and pulls out a hammer she's used for hanging pictures. She tucks her face into the crevice of her elbow and takes a swing. The window shatters. She rakes away the shards along the seal and rushes over to the nightstand. As she begins to swipe away the clutter, lamp and all, the thing beneath the bed growls loudly. Carol catches a glimpse in her peripheral of a long, bony hand reaching out from beneath the bed, aiming for Carol's ankle. She screams and jumps backwards. The thing continues to growl. Its pale fingers fall limp to the hardwood. Its nails make a loud tapping sound.

Carol hurries and places the nightstand beneath the broken window. The door thuds again as she climbs upon the nightstand.

She wiggles through the window and falls to the ground. Her hip barks in protest. She grunts and manages to get to her feet. She hears her bedroom door burst open. She doesn't turn back to look but makes a break for the grove of pines.

Running and stumbling her way into the tree line, she pushes away the swipes of bony branches. Her tender feet scream with every poke and jab from the sticks and pine needles. Her lungs burn like they've been doused with gasoline and lit to a flame. Her breath steams into the frigid air. Running between the pines, she retrieves her cell. Moments later she finds the contact she's looking for and places the call.

Panting and glancing over her shoulder, she waits for her son to answer.

TALES FROM UNCLE JOE
BLOOD IN THE SWAMP
RANDALL LANE

TALES FROM UNCLE JOE
WHEN THE BAYOU SINGS
RANDALL LANE

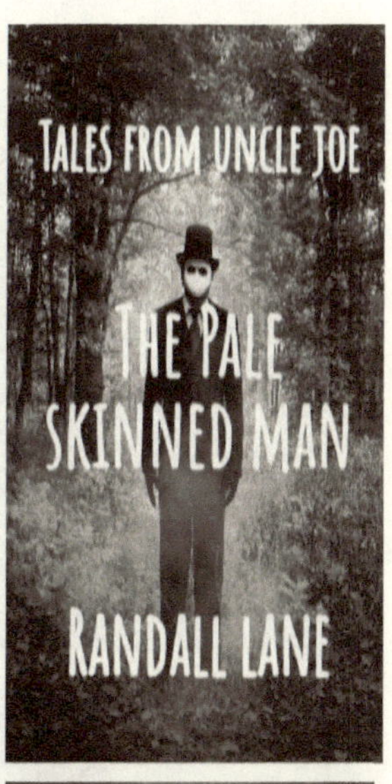
TALES FROM UNCLE JOE
THE PALE SKINNED MAN
RANDALL LANE

TALES FROM UNCLE JOE
THE MISSING
RANDALL LANE

TALES FROM UNCLE JOE
NIGHT HOWLS
RANDALL LANE

TALES FROM UNCLE JOE
NATIVE SON
RANDALL LANE

TALES FROM UNCLE JOE
MUTILATIONS
RANDALL LANE

TALES FROM UNCLE JOE
IT ROAMS AT NIGHT
RANDALL LANE

TALES FROM UNCLE JOE
AN INSIDE JOB
RANDALL LANE

Thank you once again for joining me on this journey through story. It was such a joy compiling this book of short stories. From one reader to another, may we all continue to find ourselves as we escape into the written word.

> Till next time!
> All the best,

Randall Lane